With any questions write to
Katrina Lee
The Brady Street Boys
PO Box 2155
Elkhart, IN 46515

First edition 2021

Book design by Tobi Carter and Viewfinder Creative
Illustrations by Josh Tufts

ISBN 978-1-7359035-3-8 (paperback)
ISBN 978-1-7359035-4-5 (ebook)

www.katrinahooverlee.com.

THE BRADY STREET BOYS

Book 1:
Trapped in the Tunnel

written by Katrina Hoover Lee

But the fruit of the Spirit is love, joy,
peace, longsuffering, gentleness,
goodness, faith, meekness, temperance:
against such there is no law.
Galatians 5:22-23

The Brady Street Boys
Adventure Series

Terry, Gary and Larry Fitzpatrick live in northern Indiana along the St. Joseph River. President Reagan lives in the White House. Gasoline costs 90 cents a gallon. For families like the Fitzpatricks, computers and cell phones are still things of the future. The boys' Christian parents teach them to pray and give them a project to learn the fruit of the Spirit. They help Gary navigate the pain of losing his leg and his firefighting dreams.

But having a wooden leg doesn't keep Gary from adventures. With Terry the acrobat, and Larry the brain, Gary begins a quest to find an answer to the most important mystery of all.

What happened to the surgeon who amputated Gary's leg, and has now disappeared?

Contents

1. We Don't Want to Move 1

2. A Project and a House Called Number Ten....................10

3. The Bicycle Ramp 18

4. The Mystery Map..27

5. A Strange Smell..33

6. A Row in the *London*..41

7. At the Stratford Library 49

8. What the Police Found..56

9. What the Police Did Not Find 65

10. A Nighttime Expedition 74

11. A New Assignment 84

12. A Clue and a Chore...90

13. I Write a Letter...98

14. The Second Map..104

15. Feeding Fritz...112

16. More Detective Plans.................................... 119
17. A Footprint...126
18. Things Get Strange.....................................135
19. Tina's Secret Room.....................................144
20. We Need an Ambulance............................. 154
21. We Call for Help 164
22. Help Arrives... 174
23. Raspy Tells His Story 182
24. Tina Tells Her Story...................................190

About the Author..202

CHAPTER ONE

We Don't Want to Move

We have to convince Mom this neighborhood is safe," I said to the wooden bicycle ramp I held off the garage floor.

"Uh-huh." Terry's voice came from under the ramp.

"And Dad too," Larry added, from behind the pages of a book.

"Well, sure." I shifted the weight of the ramp from one arm to the other. "But Mom is the one who worries."

Let me explain our names. My Dad's name is Ferguson Fitzpatrick. Mom's name is Arabella. The first thing they decided when they met each other was if they ever had children, they would give them short, easy names.

They went a little extreme.

1. First, Terry was born, the one building the ramp. He has done crazy things since he was born 14 years ago.
2. Then it was me, Gary, born a year later, holding the ramp so Terry could work underneath.
3. Larry, our encyclopedia, is 12.

They gave us easy names, all right. But whenever we introduce ourselves, people smile and gush like we are a bunch of babies.

"Terry, Gary, and Larry?" Their eyes widen and their tongues cluck. "Now isn't that cute?"

We escape as soon as we can.

Terry had been constructing the wooden ramp all morning with help from Larry and me. Using scraps of Dad's lumber, he hammered together a ramp that rose about three feet in the air and stretched four feet long. It was a patchwork of pieces, but he had put in so many nails that I couldn't imagine it falling apart.

Larry helped by reading out loud from his book about bicycle stunts. I helped by sketching a blueprint for him on graph paper. I also made lists of all the different things he would need. Besides rowing our boat the *London* on the river, making lists and drawing are my two favorite activities. I always carried a notebook in my pocket.

"I know Mom is the main worry person, but I bet Dad worries too." Terry, flat on his back on the cool cement of Dad's garage, poked and pulled at a loose piece of wood. "He's just not saying anything. Or maybe he just wants to drive a tractor and milk cows."

"No, he doesn't." I shifted again, hands aching. "He likes repairing boat motors more than anything."

"Living on a farm sounds fun." Larry spoke without looking up from his bicycle book.

"I don't want to live on a farm," I said. "Cows and sheep and manure and thorns."

Terry reached for Dad's hammer. It was beyond him by three feet.

"See, you like making lists." Larry looked up at me now and nodded toward my supplies list and blueprint. "You could make a farm list. Compare cows and sheep."

"Oh, stop it!" I barked. Moving was not a joke to me. If we moved away from the St. Joseph River, I could not row the *London* on its welcoming waters. "Larry, can't you put that book down for one second and give Terry the hammer?"

Red color rose in Larry's pale cheeks at my harsh tone.

He slid across the floor and kicked at the hammer. Terry is the athletic one of the three of us, not Larry. But somehow, Larry hit that hammer just right, and it shot toward Terry like a bullet.

"Yoooowwwwl!" Terry yelled as he jerked his arm in self-defense.

I dived at the hammer to keep it from sailing into Terry's head. Larry might have intelligence to spare, but Terry needs every brain cell he has.

I failed to reach the hammer in time. But in trying, I dropped the ramp. It came down with a thwack on Terry's ribs.

For a second, we were all yelling. Terry yelled from pain. I yelled at Larry again for kicking the hammer. Larry yelled at me for dropping the ramp on Terry. Then Terry yelled at both of us for our stupidity.

On the bright side, Terry had blocked the hammer with his upper arm, saving his brain.

After Terry finished yelling, the garage grew still. Terry mumbled something about brotherly love.

"What?" I asked.

"You know, Mom's project." He rubbed his upper arm. "Guess I'd better stop yelling if I'm going to make it on her chart. Although you guys should stop beating me up, too."

"It was an accident." Larry shuffled his feet on the garage floor. "Kind of."

"Sorry." I leaned against a metal barrel. "I don't want to move away from the river."

My comment made us forget about being mad at each other and brought to mind our actual problem. Across from me, Larry's book lay closed on the garage floor beside him. Terry had extricated himself from under the ramp and was now lying on top of it, feet sticking off the lower end. His head rested on the flat part at the top with his brown curls pointed toward the back of the garage.

"What if we move to a farm with no library close by?" Larry shook his head and picked the bicycle book off the floor. "That would be terrible."

Larry devoured books as if they were food and drink. When he finished one book, he started another.

"Why are you so scared about leaving the river, Gary?" Terry looked my direction. "I would miss Dad's shop more than the river."

"I guess it's because operating a boat is something I can do well with one leg." I looked at the wheelbarrow beside the ramp, my wrists resting on my good knee.

I had learned to love rowing. Dad's boat had a motor. But he thought we should learn to row before we could use the motorboat.

Now here's what I like about my brothers.

They nodded thoughtfully at my wooden leg.

They avoided thoughtless comments about all the things a person can do with one leg.

They didn't talk about how nice it is to have a wooden leg when you step into a thistle patch because you don't notice the thistles.

They understood having only one good leg bothered me a lot. Back when I had two legs, Terry, Larry and I dreamed of being firefighters when we grew up. We would run into burning buildings and drag out trapped people. We would climb trees and telephone poles and rescue stranded animals.

Then the problems began. I lost my leg above the knee, and Larry nearly died of pneumonia.

With my wooden leg, I can't run up and down stairs like I used to. I'll never be able to drag people from burning buildings and save their lives.

Larry still has breathing problems, especially in a cloud of dust. He would never survive in smoke. However, he loves books so much he doesn't seem to mind the lost dream.

But I do mind. It doesn't seem right. Only Terry can do whatever he wants.

But I can row our old aluminum boat, the *London*.

"No doubt about it." Terry stared at the garage ceiling. "You're better at rowing than I am. I don't like to admit it, but it's true."

Terry wins the award for the tallest, strongest, and most acrobatic. He throws a football farther than either Larry or I, runs faster, and does better bike stunts.

"Yup, it's true." Larry nodded, just to irritate Terry and to make me happy. "You are better at rowing than Terry."

"Hey!" Terry stretched, reaching his arms off the end of the ramp. "You don't have to agree, Larry."

It felt good. I laughed despite my fears.

I named our boat too. When I was in bed after losing my leg in surgery, I learned countries and their capitals. Mom made flashcards for me so I could learn them. She gave me a book with pictures from around the world. On the page about London, I saw an enormous tower clock. Mom said they called it Big Ben. I practiced drawing that majestic clock on the back of a hospital napkin.

As I was drawing, Mom told me what she had learned about Big Ben when she was a schoolteacher. The clock tower rises over 300 feet tall, she said, and has a bell that weighs 15 tons. Three times a week, men wind the big clock, which takes about an hour. Then Big Ben can chime hour after hour, rarely running too fast or too slow. But if Big Ben slows, they place pennies on the pendulum to change the weight. Each penny helps Big Ben gain 0.4 seconds.

When Dad got the rowboat the next summer, I thought about the big clock. I named the boat the *London*. I had thought about naming it Big Ben, but the name sounded bigger than our little rowboat. The *London* isn't fancy like Dad's motorboat. It is a simple aluminum boat with three seats, each smaller than the one behind it. Aluminum handles let us tie the boat to the dock or pull it in to shore. Small or not, I loved the *London* at first sight. I took a magic marker and wrote *London* on her stern.

"Would you like a motorboat, Gary?" Larry asked. "I mean, if Dad ever lets us get one? Or would you rather just keep using the rowboat since you're so good at that?"

"Oh, I'd be the best at running the motorboat too."

Terry sat up like a current of electricity had zapped him. He glared at me. Then with a laugh he said, "Hey, why don't you put your fancy rowing muscles to good use and help me get this ramp out for practice?"

"Did you ever tighten that loose piece?"

"Oh, right," Terry grumbled, rubbing his upper arm. "This time I'm going to flip the ramp over rather than trust you to hold it for me."

With a few strokes of the hammer, he declared it finished.

"Where are you putting the ramp?" Larry backed away as Terry and I carried the wooden structure into the warmth of the June sun.

"Back yard?" I blinked my eyes, adjusting to the brightness.

"What, you want me to fall in the river?" Terry scowled.

"Yes, yes!" Larry clapped his hands. "You could do a flip on your way over the bank."

"And see if you can land bike first."

Terry rolled his eyes.

Our back yard isn't much bigger than a bathtub. Our favorite maple tree and a metal clothesline take up most of the space. Then the yard drops away to the river and wooden stairs lead down to the *London*'s dock. No matter how we positioned the ramp back there, Terry could somersault into the river.

"It's so hot it would be fun to get wet." Terry marched toward the street. "But I need to perfect my skills on a flat surface first."

Our front yard was flat, but again too small. Mom's yellow marigolds lined the walk from the street to the front porch, cutting the front yard in half. We knew better than to ride a bicycle through Mom's flowers. So the only other option was the street.

We had good reasons for our choice.

1. Few cars drive down Brady Street.
2. Even if a car came, Terry would escape in time.
3. Even if a car hit Terry, he would be okay.

We're all good at surviving tough times. I already told you that Larry almost died when he was little. Mom told me I would have died of cancer if the doctor had not cut off my leg.

And Terry? Well, Terry breaks one bone per year on average, and he has always recovered from every accident. So we dragged the wooden ramp out into the middle of Brady Street, between our house and the empty house we call Number Ten.

Number Ten is the reason for all our problems. It's the reason Mom thinks we should move to a different place.

What's wrong with Number Ten? Well, we don't know if the house is actually empty.

CHAPTER TWO

A Project and a House Called Number Ten

I need to tell you a little bit about our mom.

Since we are all boys, Mom is the only girl in the family. She has the same features as Larry: bright yellow hair and blue eyes. All three of us love our mom a lot.

But, even though we love our mom, there are a few problems.

First, because she used to be a teacher, she gives us assignments, even in the summer. *Especially* in the summer.

Second, she helps manage the charity garden across the road from us. Mom makes us help sometimes, pulling weeds or picking tomatoes so that poor people can get enough to eat. If you've never tried picking tomatoes before, don't try it. It's hard work.

Third, Mom worries about us. I guess I can't blame her since Larry and I almost died when we were younger. And Terry almost dies most years.

Back to the projects. Why did I memorize capitals when I was seven years old? Assignments. And she made it so fun, I thought it was a game. I also thought it was normal. Surely all children would know the capitals of Kenya and Finland and Spain.

So now, even though it's summer vacation, Mom designed a project for us. Not only is it a project, but it's a nine-part project, meant to last nine weeks. She told Dad about it, and of course he thought it was a fantastic idea.

"Okay, boys," Dad said from his recliner just a few nights ago. "We have a project for you during vacation. It's easy, and it will help you learn about the fruit of the Spirit."

We eyed Dad suspiciously. Larry looked over the top of his book. Terry, on the floor, looked up from a complex Lego creation. I paused in my study of the Rubik's cube.

None of us had any problem learning from the Bible. We were used to going to church every Sunday. We understood the Spirit was part of God. But we didn't like that word. *Project*. It sounded too much like school. Also, we knew Dad didn't come up with projects like this.

"Oh, we already know the fruits of the Spirit." Terry flopped onto his back on the carpet of the living room floor. He waved his hand in the air as if to wave away the project. "We learned those in Sunday school years ago."

Terry's favorite chair is the floor. He loves stretching out on the floor, summer or winter, spring or fall.

"Apparently you don't." Mom looked up from a poster board, marker in hand. "Because it is *fruit* of the Spirit, not *fruits* of the Spirit." Terry groaned, but Mom went right on. "So can you name all nine?"

"Oh, sure." Larry put down his book to begin his recitation.

Yes. My body relaxed against the couch and I focused confidently on the Rubik's cube again. *Larry knows everything. He will impress Mom by reciting them all, and then she won't make us do the project after all.*

"Love, joy, peace..." Larry stopped and tapped his forehead.

What? Surely Larry couldn't be running out of options already.

"Long-suffering?" I said shakily. This was not going well. I had been counting on Larry to rattle off the fruits, and he had stopped after only three. The same three I knew.

"Okay." Terry rolled back over and picked up his Lego project. "So we don't know them. What do we have to do?"

"You don't have to if you *want* to," Dad said.

That's his favorite phrase whenever we are complaining about work.

"I'm making a chart." Mom drew a long line on the poster. "We're going to find these nine qualities in other people and in ourselves."

"Oh, come on!" Terry said. That's one of his favorite phrases. "This is a nine-part project?"

"One for each week of vacation," Mom said. "We'll start this week with the first fruit, which is love. At suppertime, we'll discuss if we showed love to anyone or if anyone showed love to us. You need to each provide an example for the chart each week. Then we'll come up with something that symbolizes that fruit. That's it."

"That's it?" Terry tore several blocks off his design. "That's like a summer-long research paper."

"Can we symbolize the fruit with actual fruit?" I twisted a row of blocks on the Rubik's cube. "Love is like an apple."

"How is love like an apple?" Mom's marker suspended in the air as she looked up at me.

"Never mind," I sighed.

"Just one example and one symbol?" Larry turned back to his book. "That's not too bad."

"It would be bad if you had brothers like mine," Terry mumbled.

Larry and I just shook our heads. We didn't even bother commenting.

"So, we start with love." Dad picked up his newspaper. "Keep an eye out for acts of love and try to use that fruit yourself."

So that was that. We had a summer-long project to find fruit of the Spirit.

I also need to tell you about Number Ten. The house we thought was empty.

First, let me tell you about the Brady Street neighborhood. Across from our house, an immense garden spreads over all four lots. This is the garden Mom helps manage. So we don't have any close neighbors there, unless you count the green squash plants that wave at us in the breeze.

Then there is our side of the street. There used to be a house between us and Lexington Avenue, but the owner knocked the house down before I was born. Now shrubs and tall grass and a cluster of trees clutter the lot and muffle the sound of traffic from the busy avenue.

Our house is next.

After our house, is the empty house we call Number Ten.

Right past Number Ten is Tina's wooden fence with a kayak tied to it. And then there is Tina's house, with a bronze owl statue staring at passersby from its perch on the bottom porch step. Neighbor Tina walks around the garden with her Rottweiler.

After that, the park. It's not much of a park, just two rusting basketball hoops with torn nets and a tennis court with no net. That's it.

After the park, the river curves in. And that's all of Brady Street. An alley curls along the back of the garden, connecting the park to the next street. Sometimes people walk or drive down the alley to play in the park. But, besides a few volunteers who work the garden, few cars visit our street.

Until last fall, we had quiet neighbors who lived in Number Ten. We called it Number Ten because someone had placed

the address numbers 410 on the front door. Then the 4 fell off, and it was just 10.

White paint flaked from the siding. The front steps sagged. The porch railing had lost a spindle, like a smile with a missing tooth.

We didn't know our neighbors well. Mom took them a plate of her famous chocolate peanut butter cookies and they barely thanked her. But I remember their little girl running after a yellow balloon last fall. It was a crisp autumn day, and our maple tree was brilliant red and her balloon floated away into the tree. I rescued it for her, and it made me wish I knew her better.

Her quiet mother kept a white angel in the flowerbed out front. The angel played on a flute and had gold-edged wings. It looked like a Christmas angel. But Mom said there was nothing wrong with keeping an angel in a flowerbed all year. Also, Mom said, it took much less care than the marigolds and geraniums and peonies we had.

The little girl's father mowed the lawn most weeks. When a big shrub began to sag in the front of the house, the man tied it to the porch railing with a blue plastic string. The string kept the green bush from falling onto the lawn.

Dad smiled when he saw the blue string. "I like people with creative ideas."

Mom would not have wanted the ceramic angel in her flowerbed. Dad would not have tied a shrub to our house. But our parents told us that every human being is important. Even if people did things that seemed strange to us, we were not allowed to make fun of anyone.

Then, just before Thanksgiving, our quiet neighbors moved away. A "For Sale" sign appeared on the front lawn. The grass grew wild with no one to cut it. When snow came in January, the shrub bent low and the blue string snapped. In spring, the weeds exploded, along with the fresh green growth of the grass.

All that happened before the trouble started.

One day during school, Mom saw a group of five men go into the house. Was someone moving in? Maybe. But the men had no boxes or furniture.

Besides, the men didn't look like investors or landlords. They had long, dirty hair and rumpled clothes and bandanas tied around their foreheads.

"That old man who comes to the food pantry was with them." Mom's forehead creased in concern.

"Raspy?" Terry forced another bite of grilled fish. Mom had made it because Dad loved it. Terry couldn't stand fish.

Mom nodded. She looked at Terry as if she was trying to decide whether to laugh.

"He talks in a raspy voice." Terry imitated him.

"I guess. But don't forget that he has a name. Carl."

"Do you think they were breaking in?" Dad squeezed a section of lemon and watched the drops fall onto his fillet.

"I don't know." Mom forked up a flaky bite of white fish and sighed.

And that's when she said the words that terrified us.

"Ferguson, maybe it's time we take up your mom's offer and move to Iowa. The farm would do the boys good."

CHAPTER THREE

The Bicycle Ramp

But I refused to think about moving. There was bicycle jumping to do. Terry was the only one planning to do the jump. But both Larry and I had plenty of tasks to record his acrobatics.

Like I mentioned, Brady Street slopes down off busy Lexington Avenue. Terry wanted to start close to the top of Brady Street to get up speed. The wooden ramp sat on the bottom of the slope, where the road leveled out as it passed our house, then Number Ten, and finally Mrs. Tina's house with the bronze owl.

Larry agreed to hold a yardstick so we could estimate Terry's air height and how far the bicycle flew before touching down. I waited with graph paper and pen to write Larry's numbers. I also held my stopwatch, the cord looped around my neck, ready to measure Terry's air time as well. We were pretty sure if we did our measurements right, we could calculate his speed.

We were making final adjustments to the ramp, when a voice spoke behind us.

"Hello, boys! What a clever contraption. Did you make it?"

We whirled around.

A man with red hair, red eyebrows, and a red mustache grinned at us. He carried a leather bag over one shoulder.

"I don't mean to startle you." His lips curled in a half smile. "My name's Benjamin. Just doing a little research for my antique business."

When he said the letter *b*, it seemed to burst out of his mouth like a minor explosion.

"You are an antique dealer?" Larry's blue eyes lit up.

"Yes, indeed. I am. Interesting, isn't it? But I need some help. I had a customer years ago who came to my shop and bought an old clock. He said he had a friend who lived by the river and might have one of the rare Braggit clocks. Now, I have a client who runs a museum. And he wants a Braggit clock. The problem is, I forgot to get the exact address. Do you boys know of anyone close by who likes antique clocks?"

We had all been staring at Benjamin's brilliant red hair.

"I think Tina's husband used to work at a clock company." Larry looked at me, and then at Terry, for support. "What kind of clock did you say?"

"Braggit," Benjamin said.

"How's it spelled?" Larry asked. "Gary, write it in your book."

"Hmmm," Benjamin said. "Let's say B-R-A-G-G-I-T."

"Tina's husband is not living anymore," I added after writing the word. "I doubt she knows anything about clocks, especially not a rare kind."

"She's just a grouchy old lady with a big Rottweiler dog who will bite the head off anyone who gets too close," Terry added.

The man smiled. "Okay, no problemo." He snapped open the leather bag and pulled out a sheet of paper. "Let me show you a copy of this map." Under the lines the copy machine had made, we saw a crude drawing.

"Are those houses?" Terry pointed to boxes sketched on the paper alongside a squiggly line.

"I guess maybe so?" the dealer said. "This customer was fascinating, quite fascinating. He said the map was from a book about the Underground Railroad. And it was from this friend who owned the Braggit clock."

"Oh!" Larry stared at the map. "That's interesting. What did the Underground Railroad have to do with the clocks?"

"Oh, maybe nothing." The red-haired man laughed. "But you know these history people. They love anything old. You're one of those history people, aren't you?" He poked Larry in the shoulder.

Larry laughed and flushed red for the second time that day. Since his hair is whitish-yellow, his face looks even redder.

"Larry reads everything." Terry rolled his eyes. "History, geography, stories, encyclopedias."

"I can tell," Benjamin chirped. "Well, I'll continue on my search. Larry the historian, would you like a copy of this map?"

"Sure!" Larry beamed, taking the map. "Thanks."

"All right then, I'll be off." The antique dealer waved. He headed up the street on foot toward Lexington Avenue, where cars zipped by above us.

We exchanged glances.

"That was interesting." Larry carefully folded the map and put it in his pocket.

"And a little weird." I glanced at the man's fiery head fading away up the street.

"And an interruption." Terry yanked his bike around to face the hill. "I vote we don't tell Mom about him either. He was okay, but a little strange. And she doesn't need to hear about any more strange people in our neighborhood."

"I'm kind of glad he didn't go talk to Tina," Larry said. His thin fingers tightened around the yard stick. Everything about him is thin: his fingers, his yellow hair, and his intelligent voice.

Terry mounted his bicycle and rode up the hill, his curls like a forest of springs. By the time Terry turned his bicycle to face us, the red-haired man had disappeared behind the trees in the empty lot.

Mom always said she liked those trees. If it weren't for that little patch of woods, she said, she would feel like she lived in a busy town. But the trees shielded us from the sounds and smells of traffic.

I thought about the red-haired antique dealer. Perhaps I was just imagining things. But there were a few oddities.

1. He had no vehicle.
2. He apparently had come from that park, or Tina's house, or Number Ten, or maybe from across the garden. We had been facing Lexington Avenue, so we knew he didn't come that way.
3. His hair was such a shocking red.

"Did that man dye his hair?" I asked Larry. "Didn't it seem like a really odd red color?"

"Benjamin? I don't know." Larry clearly hadn't thought of his hair, too busy being impressed by his job description. "Look, here comes Terry."

Terry rose up on his bicycle, shoulders hunched forward. His curls shot out behind his head like rocket smoke. His shirt plastered to his body.

"Wa-aa-aa-aa-hooo!" Terry yelled as he rode up the ramp. As the bike left the ramp, I clicked "start" on my stopwatch. It rose into the air gloriously, crested, and fell. Terry expertly landed on his back wheel, and I clicked "stop."

"That was 0.78 seconds of air time," I hollered to Terry.

I wrote the figure in the first row on my graph paper and labeled the row "Jump."

"Ten feet of distance," Larry announced from his knees in the road. "I didn't get a good estimate of height. Nice jump, though."

"Going again!" Terry shouted, pedaling furiously up the street.

Terry made three successful jumps with no disasters. He sailed in for the fourth jump, crouched low, brown eyes locked on the target, hands lightly gripping the handlebars, face flushed and sweaty. I was sitting in the grass at the edge of the street. Behind Terry, I saw a police car turn off Lexington Avenue and onto Brady Street.

"Wa-aa-aa-aa-hooo!" Terry couldn't see the police car coming up behind him.

We had to get the ramp off the road so the policeman could get to the bad people. I forgot to push start on the stopwatch. Instead, I jumped up and ran into the street.

I should have timed my movements better, because somehow I got Terry off-balance by running in so suddenly.

"Yaaaa-oooooowwwwlllll!" Terry yelled. He shot off the ramp, bicycle wobbling.

Since I reached down to grab the ramp, I missed seeing Terry landing on his front wheel and somersaulting—not on purpose—over his handlebars. Behind me, a bicycle clattered and a body thumped to the street.

I turned around in time to see Terry rolling over, so I knew he was alive.

"Terry, get off the street so the policeman can pass." I grabbed the ramp as I yelled, dragging it to the curb.

Instead of passing, the officer pulled into the lane in front of our garage. He got out, nodded to me and strode over to Terry.

"Everything all right here?" he asked.

Terry shook himself and sat up, blood trailing down his right forearm.

"Yes, I'm fine," Terry gasped.

"Are your parents home? I'm Officer Jackson."

"Mom is." I gaped at the officer, stopwatch still at the ready. Was it a crime to fall off a bicycle?

Larry stood behind me, holding the yardstick.

Turns out, Terry, Larry, and I *were* the bad people the officer was after.

Officer Jackson walked down the cement path to our porch, between the rows of marigolds. He climbed the four steps and knocked on the door.

Mom opened it. Her eyes flew wide.

"No worries, ma'am." He tipped his cap to her. "Did you know that your boys were playing in the middle of the street?"

"I did not know, officer." A red flush colored her face up to her yellow hair.

"We had a concerned neighbor call in," the police officer said. "It would be safest if they would play... another place. I believe one just had a spill as I drove up."

I didn't bother mentioning that Terry's spill was the officer's fault. If Officer Jackson hadn't driven in, I wouldn't have run to pull the ramp out of the middle of the road. If I hadn't run up to the ramp, I wouldn't have distracted Terry and got him off-balance. If he hadn't gotten off-balance, he wouldn't have landed on his front tire nor made the unfortunate somersault.

Thankfully, the bike appeared to be okay. Terry wheeled it off to the side. Even the chain turned normally on its sprockets.

Actually, I take back what I said. It wasn't the officer's fault. It was our grouchy old neighbor Tina's fault. She's our only neighbor, so she must have tattled on us.

"Don't worry," Mom assured the policeman. "It will certainly not happen again."

CHAPTER FOUR

The Mystery Map

Terry, blood dripping from his arm, biked away from the scene as if he could not bear to hear more. He rode to the park and turned behind the garden, where the trees hid him.

Larry collected his book and yardstick. I still had my stopwatch around my neck, but I yanked the ramp up into the grass and flopped beside it on my stomach, staring at the green blades.

"What about a world where people look like their character?" Larry's voice broke into my solitude.

I jumped. The wooden ramp blocked my view of Larry, and I hadn't noticed him sit down on the other side.

"What on earth are you talking about?"

Larry chuckled. I imagined his blue eyes full of delight at my confusion.

"I feel like Charles Dickens." Grass blades crunched as if he were sitting up. "I'm going to write a book someday. And I'm thinking of writing a book where people look like their character."

"Oh, so if I was really perfect, I would grow my leg back? Is that what you mean?"

At this, I heard Larry shuffling and pretty soon something that sounded like two elbows knocked on the wooden ramp. Sure enough, when I flipped to my back, I found Larry's eyes looking straight at me under his thin yellow hair.

"No. If you were good, you would be *strikingly* handsome." Larry flourished his hand in the air as he exaggerated the word *strikingly*.

"Thanks for saying I'm not handsome."

It was true. Besides my wooden leg, I'm just kind of normal. I don't read encyclopedias like Larry or risk my life on stunts like Terry. Even my hair is normal: brown and straight. Everyone talks about Terry's curly hair, and Larry's yellow hair, but no one has ever remarked on mine. Well, occasionally someone calls me handsome. But the only thing they stare at on me is my bad leg. They watch me like they are police detectives, trying to figure out why I'm limping.

I looked back at Larry.

"But why on earth don't you just give me my leg back if you're making up this story, anyway? Come on, Larry, doesn't it ever drive you crazy? Your breathing troubles. And me missing a leg. And neither of us able to be firefighters, no matter how much we want to be."

Larry shifted off his elbows, sat in the grass, and pulled the ramp out of our way. With the ramp gone, I could see the empty porch. I hadn't bothered to watch Officer Jackson leave or watch Mom go into the house.

I guess I was mad at a few people.

1. Those five bandana-wearing men that came into Number Ten and scared Mom so badly she thought of moving.
2. Our neighbor Tina for calling the police on us.
3. That surgeon who cut my leg off.

We didn't talk about this much. Larry pinched his lips together, as if thinking deeply.

"Sometimes I think about how glad I am to be alive." Larry's blue eyes wandered down the long rows of squash plants across the road. "Mom and Dad said that I almost died. Didn't you almost die too? Wouldn't you have died if they hadn't cut off your leg?"

"Yes, but how do I know that?" I felt my hand yanking on a clump of grass, tearing the blades from their stems. "You read in that book last winter about the doctors who cut off someone's leg, and then they found out it was the wrong person. What if my doctor cut off my leg but it really wasn't necessary?"

I remembered winning a foot race in first grade. But I tried not to think too much about that. It hurt to think about running on two legs. I had thought I was used to the idea of having a wooden leg. Used to the idea of never becoming a firefighter. But somehow this talk about moving away from the river had me fighting mad about it. And the doctor seemed like the perfect person to blame.

Larry's head turned like a puppet on a string. His eyes burned into mine.

"Those were crazy accidents I was reading about. Why would you think your doctor in Chicago was like that?"

"I don't know." I grabbed another fistful of grass. "I guess I've just been thinking too much about moving."

"We will not move." Larry looked at me patiently, like he would at a toddler. "We'll prove to Mom it's safe to live here."

I squeezed my eyes shut. My insides felt like exploding. I just shook my head.

"Besides, Gary, people like us understand better how Jesus suffered on the cross. We know a little about suffering."

Paper rattled above me.

I sighed. Larry always had the right answers.

"I'm sure you're right."

"Come on, Gary, I don't know where Terry biked off to. But help me evaluate this map."

"Okay, fine." I sat up.

I didn't want to study an old map. But I knew that Larry was trying to get my mind on something else. I made a mental note to remember Larry for Mom's chart about people who show love. On the inside, I still boiled, but I pushed the anger away.

Larry smoothed the map on the bicycle ramp and pulled it closer. I sat up and looked at it with him.

Right away, I noticed three things:

1. The squiggly line at the side must be the St. Joseph River.
2. If it was, then the four boxes on the map were likely houses on our street.
3. There were lines between the boxes, as if showing paths from one house to the next.

"Those are houses." I said, excited despite myself. "And this is the river."

"Well, it can't be our street then. We only have three houses."

I pointed past Dad's garage.

"Now there are only three. That overgrown lot used to have a house on it."

Larry looked down at the map as if he expected it to talk.

"So... you think the mapmaker made this before that house was taken down." Larry looked up at me with question marks written in his eyes.

"Sure," I said. "Didn't he say it was years ago that he got this map?"

Larry frowned. "He mentioned the Underground Railroad. *That* was a long time ago."

"Like when slaves were escaping and all that, right?" It's a pity. Larry is the youngest of us three, but whenever we have questions about history, we ask him.

"Right. People in the North would help them get to freedom. Hide them in secret rooms, things like that."

We puzzled over the map.

"Maybe this person with the famous clock lives in a house used by the Underground Railroad." I pulled more grass, this time to assist my detective work rather than my anger. "Since the house has secret rooms, the clock person has a place to store his antiques where no one will see them."

Larry's eyes widened the longer I talked.

"You should be a detective. But did the Underground Railroad even operate in Indiana? I thought it was only closer to the Southern states. And this map could be from some totally different river."

"Huh, I have no idea." I shrugged, but Larry's praise pleased me. "But Red Hair thinks it belongs here somewhere."

"Let's go to the library." Larry brightened. "I want to find that clock maker. Breaking? Breynet? What was his name?"

I pulled my notebook out of my pocket. "He told me it was B-R-A-G-G-I-T."

"Penny can help us." Larry snapped his fingers. "And I want to know if the Underground Railroad was in our neighborhood."

"Did they actually hide people underground?"

"No, of course not." Larry rolled his eyes. "It just means hidden."

CHAPTER FIVE

A Strange Smell

A screech of bicycle brakes announced Terry's return. He dismounted, red-faced.

I couldn't tell if the redness was from riding hard. Or from anger. Or because it was summer and late afternoon and just plain hot.

"When will Tina keep to her own business?" Terry threw himself into the grass.

Honestly, Terry, Larry, and I don't usually all agree on anything except for Mom's Saturday night homemade pizza. But this afternoon, we agreed.

Neighbor Tina should mind her own business.

I don't even want to talk about Tina. But you should know a few things.

1. Tina complains constantly about living in the United States. She says she wishes she would have stayed in Germany.
2. Tina's Rottweiler looks like it could eat a compact car.
3. Dad makes us mow Tina's lawn since her husband died. But she doesn't pay us.

I don't like Tina bossing us and complaining about Germany. But I'll mow Tina's lawn without complaining if we can just stay by the river.

Could we find another river like our very own St. Joseph's? One with a dock full of knot holes to drop things through? One conveniently near the library and Dad's repair shop? No, never.

"Tina could move back to Germany," Larry suggested cheerfully from his perch on the top end of the ramp.

I shook my head. "Dad says she's been saying she hates the United States for the last twenty years. She isn't going anywhere."

"Well, let me do a few jumps on the bicycle ramp here." Terry got up off the grass.

"Oh, since the blood on your arm has dried, you're ready to go again?" Sometimes I just don't understand how he keeps going.

"Yup!" Terry grabbed his bicycle. "I won't be able to get up enough speed to fall into the river. I may as well go that direction."

Whoever built our house and Number Ten put the houses way too close to each other. It's kind of ridiculous because both lots have extra room on the opposite sides. But between the houses, there is only about ten feet of space. Plenty of space to walk through, but not a lot of extra space for bicycle stunts.

The river wound below us just twenty feet beyond. But Terry was sure he could brake before he flew over the bank, since he wouldn't be going fast.

And he was right. He didn't fly into the river. He flew, but not that way.

Larry got off the ramp, and we all helped position it. Terry backed off to the sidewalk to pick up speed. I walked about ten feet past the ramp for the best view of Terry's wheels touching down. I held my stopwatch, ready to hit the start button.

We missed a few details.

1. Grass can be a little slippery.
2. No one noticed the garden hose in the grass before the ramp.
3. Number Ten has two glass basement windows.

Before I had time to press the start button on the stopwatch, I saw that Terry's bike was rising up the ramp almost completely sideways. We realized later that the reason for this was the nearly hidden garden hose. I am not a scientist like Larry, but I know when a flying object is about to strike. I dived from my seat near the abandoned house toward Mom's peony bed beside our house.

For those of you who have never dived into a bed of peonies, let me explain. Peonies are huge pink and purple flowers on tall green stems, and they almost always have fuzzy bumblebees bumbling around in them.

Huge purple petals flashed past. Stems popped. An angry bumblebee buzzed. A sharp pain burned on my upper arm. A bumblebee sting.

As the bumblebee stung me, I heard glass breaking and the thud of Terry's body slamming against the abandoned house. A split second later, I heard the crunching noise of the bike settling.

Mom's kitchen window looks out over the peony bed and the empty house, and she saw it all happen. In seconds, she appeared from the front porch with the first aid kit. She kept the kit within easy reach in the same way that most people keep tissues handy.

After Mom wiped the blood off Terry's forehead, we saw he had only three minor gashes. He had no broken bones, so it hardly counted as an accident.

Mom placed bandages on Terry's wounds. "You have a huge scrape on your arm and now you have gashes on your head. This ramp is going away."

"Aw, come on!" Terry winced as Mom applied a bandage. "Surely not. Just one more chance now that I know what not to do."

"What not to do?" Mom turned to me and squeezed a little antibiotic cream on the bee sting. "Biking up a ramp is what you should not do."

"Aw, come on!" Terry had a better idea this time. "Won't you show me some love and let me do it one more time—you know, like our fruit of the Spirit project?"

"Yes," Mom replied coolly. "I am showing you love— by taking the ramp away."

Too bad for Terry. He picked a clever time to remember the assignment. But it didn't help his case.

"What is that terrible smell?" Mom has the best nose of anyone I know.

"I smell it too." Larry stuck his thin nose in the air and sniffed.

I smelled nothing but peonies for a while, as I lay beside the bed, my arm burning. Mom's cream helped, so I got up. Away from the flower bed, the awful smell hit me.

"Something died." Mom turned toward the basement window.

We all stared at the window, broken remnants of glass still clinging to the old wooden frame.

"What could it be?" Larry asked. "Let me go get my book on animal skeletons."

"No." Mom dropped the antibiotic cream back into the plastic box. "We are all going inside. Larry, you can make a pitcher of grape drink since you are the only one with no injuries."

Larry is also the only one who could survive on his own cooking.

"I could get Larry's flashlight and look into the basement." Terry spoke stiffly around the bandages.

"Absolutely not," Mom said. "I am going to talk to your father, but I am thinking of calling that police officer back to check it for us."

Ah, yes. The smell had Mom worried. Again.

"What if that—" Mom snapped shut the plastic latch on the first aid kit. "It just makes me uneasy. We'll talk to Dad."

Even though we all insisted we weren't scared of what had happened in the empty house, Mom's words made us wonder.

"Could someone have died down there?" Larry asked as he stepped over the row of marigolds onto the front walk. His blue eyes, which always looked big, nearly popped out of their sockets.

"I doubt it." Terry moved his lips as little as possible. One gash came close to his mouth. "You know how Mom gets nervous about every little thing. Why would no one have reported a death?"

"I can give you a list of reasons," I said. "What if someone killed someone else? Or killed themselves? You know that's what Mom was thinking. And now she has probably decided that we need to move."

"That's not a list, Gary." Larry climbed the porch steps, his thin fingers trailing the white railing. "That's only two things, both unlikely."

A paint chip fell away from Larry's hand. Mom had told us that the next person to get into trouble needed to give the porch a fresh coat of paint.

"Say," Larry added, "have either of you seen Raspy lately?"

Terry stopped, inches from the door, and spun around.

"You think Raspy died in that house?"

"That's not what he said," I yelled. "He just asked if anyone has seen him. I haven't."

The three of us entered the house.

Raspy wandered the streets of our town. He begged for food or work to make money to buy more cigars.

Now, Mom had seen him with the strange characters marching into Number Ten. What was he up to?

Even though Raspy kept questionable company, Mom and Dad both insisted that we treat him with respect.

"We have to try to understand people," Dad said. "But we don't want you to live the same way Raspy does."

"God made every human in His image," Mom said. "Whether they take a bath once a day or once a year."

Oh, yeah. That's the other thing about Raspy. Phew! He smells so bad. Sometimes Mom lets him step inside while she makes him a sandwich. One of those times, Larry and I were up in our room. We hadn't heard him come in, but we smelled something. We tried to figure out what the smell was, and then Mom said, "Here you go, Carl. Have a great day."

As soon as the front door slammed, Mom called to us from below.

"Boys. Why were you talking about the smell when you knew Carl might hear you?"

Larry and I trudged to the head of the stairs as if we were headed to court to stand before a judge.

"We didn't know he was here," I said.

I think Mom was truly relieved to find out we weren't that mean.

But now, I didn't want to think about Raspy. His gang of men threatened our peace and happiness.

We might have to move. Leave the river. Leave the *London*.

Besides, watching my brothers climb the stairs reminded me what they had that I didn't have: two good legs.

I needed some time on the water. Now. The *London* and the river, my two friends.

CHAPTER SIX

A Row in the *London*

I raced into the house through the sitting room, the library, and the kitchen.

"Where are you heading, Gary?" Mom never misses a thing.

"To the boat." My words squeaked. I fled out the back door, something big and nasty expanding inside my chest.

Mom came after me. "Gary, what's up?"

I stopped under the maple tree, reaching up into the low-hanging leaves. I pulled off a handful.

"I just hate that doctor." I looked up into the dark interior of the tree. The sun reflected in the tree's top, far above.

"What doctor? You mean the surgeon who amputated your leg?"

"Yes." I tore the leaves into shreds in my hands. "I need to get out in the *London*."

"Okay," she said. "But talk to me first. I know it's not fair that you had to lose your leg, Gary. But I'm afraid we would have lost *you* if we hadn't done that."

"But how do you know?" My hands mashed the green leaf pieces.

Usually, Terry was the one who lost his mind. This time, it was me. Yelling into a tree, for crying out loud.

"Do you remember your roommate who died?" Mom's blue eyes and yellow hair glowed in the sunlight.

I turned back to my friend the maple tree, trying to forget the pale boy in the hospital bed across from me.

"Yes." I plucked another leaf. "But would I have died?"

"The chances are yes," said Mom. "In the 1970s, just before your surgery, only one out of every ten people who got that cancer survived even with treatment. Treatments improved by 1981, but still most people died. You were too young to understand. But I was sure you would die."

Silence covered the backyard like a fog. Above us, the maple tree tossed its leaves in the fitful breeze. Behind me, the river stretched like an old friend, who made it comfortable to have only one leg. Above the river, a pickup truck rumbled over the bridge on Lexington Street. A train horn. A bird calling. *The rippling of the river.*

"Can I go on a quick spin on the *London*?"

"Sure, if you aren't careless. Let's talk some more later. I have an idea."

"An idea?"

"Just something I want to check."

I turned to go.

"And, Gary? Talk to God about it. Tell Him how angry you are feeling right now. God can speak to us when we are completely honest with Him."

"Okay."

The back screen door opened and Larry stuck his head out.

"What you doing, Gary?"

"Going for a lap with the *London*."

"Oh, me too." Larry clasped his hands together. "I want to go the library."

Mom looked at me as if to see whether I wanted company.

Before she could speak, Terry's head stuck out the door, covered in bandages.

"Me too," he said.

I wanted to argue and tell them I was going by myself. But trips on the river are more exciting with them.

"Your face." I looked at Terry, pointing a finger.

He blinked at me like a pirate, his eye surrounded with bruises, bandages, and dried blood.

"So? I'll just stop off at the shop and help Dad clean up."

It was still two hours before supper time, so Mom agreed to our trip. She was going to make Terry stay home, but when he promised to go only to Dad's shop, she agreed.

"Let's get ice cream from the shop by the library." Larry cast a glance at Mom.

She raised a blond eyebrow. "Just a small cone. If you have money left."

"You guys always get ice cream without me," Terry said. But we all knew that Dad kept a freezer full of ice cream bars at his shop too.

Terry just likes to complain.

By the time I retrieved my money, they had both climbed into the boat. I leaped from step to wooden step down the bank on my good leg. Easier than taking each step with my wooden leg. Then I jumped into the *London*, balanced myself, and took my seat on the middle bench.

Larry sat on the small bench in the front. Terry folded himself into a bandaged heap on the wide bench in the stern. He settled his battered head on a rolled-up picnic blanket Mom had made him bring along. Larry undid the rope. I pushed off the dock with my oar, and the boat slowly eased into the river.

"I feel like a pirate." Larry dipped his hand into the water, showering an arc of drops toward the dock. "Dip yer paddles. She's a thang of beauty, maties!" He had read a pirate book last winter and shot our household full of riddles and pirate talk.

I pulled the boat into deeper water. Rowing is hard work, but it makes me come alive. I love the roughness of wood in my palms and the strength of the river pulsing up through the oars.

We passed Number Ten from the back side. I watched it, checking for activity, as if a shady person might waft out of the stinking basement. The house crouched on the bank like a lonely monster, broken and tired. A tree had fallen on the back porch in the spring, biting off the porch roof and part of the railing. Tar paper flapped from

the roof. Tall weeds and untrimmed bushes hid the steps leading up to the porch. Bigger trees close to the river soon concealed the old house.

Now we passed Tina's place. Down by the river, a bright green boat garage flashed sunlight at us. It had belonged to Tina's husband, Herbert. We hadn't seen the boat often, because Tina kept it locked inside the garage, even though Herbert was no longer living. But we knew it was a sleek, beautiful boat, with a motor.

On the bank, the wooden dog fence wrapped around the house like a mask. Above the brown slats of fence, we could see the second and third floors of the huge old house. I imagined Tina peering out the window, to see if we were misbehaving.

"Better hustle, Gary." Terry mumbled from inside his bandages. "If Tina sees us, she'll probably report us to the police for playing in the middle of the river."

I needed all my breath to row, so I didn't reply. Coming home would be easier, but now I was pulling against the current.

Passing Tina's house, the river curved. I sat backwards in the boat to make rowing easier, but over my shoulder, I got a glimpse of Dad's shop out ahead.

Coming around the bend of the St. Joseph River and seeing Dad's shop over my shoulder always thrilled me. When we started from our dock, nothing but trees and fences and a few houses lined the banks. But after the bend, we could see the village of Stratford. Dad's shop, Rocky's Riverside Restaurant, apartment buildings, a car wash, and, far away down the river, the top of a hospital in the larger city of Elkhart.

Since Terry was the oldest, he was the one who helped Dad at the shop. Larry and I disliked being left out.

"I absolutely can't have all of you at once," Dad said. "I need my shop to be standing the next day. We'll let Terry learn how to help first, since he's oldest."

I wasn't sure about his logic. The quickest way to ruin anything was to let Terry get close. Just ask the basement window. But, so far, the shop had survived all of Terry's visits. And this time, Larry and I had money in our pockets for cones, which both of us liked better than ice cream bars.

As we neared Dad's dock, I let the boat coast, dipping the paddles first on one side, then the other, to direct our landing. We bumped against the dock, and Larry caught one post with his rope. I grabbed the wood planks farther back to keep the boat parallel.

"Okay, see you guys." Terry untangled his tall body and climbed out of his seat. As he leaped to the dock, Larry pulled the rope free, and I released the planks.

"Hey, there's Harold." Terry ran toward the shop, bandages and all.

"Are we picking you up afterwards?" I hollered. "Or are you coming on Dad's boat?"

"Coming with Dad." He dashed off to chat with his new friend.

Terry had told us about Harold, a new customer who owned several fast motorboats. Intrigued with the process of boat motor repair, Harold had stayed for a while on his first visit to the shop, chatting with Dad and Terry. Harold trimmed trees for a living. Terry admired anyone with a job that involved heights, balance, saws, falling limbs, and risk of death. And he also loved fast boats.

Now I pointed our bow toward the bridge on Main Street, with its flags and lamp posts. Just beyond the bridge, we could see the wooden dock in front of the ice cream shop. In a few minutes the *London* slid under the bridge and we tied up at the dock.

1. We don't worry about the boat getting stolen.
2. We tie it up by the ice cream store, and employees are nearby all day.
3. Our boat is an old aluminum shell without a motor. We love it, but no one else wants it.

Larry and I decided to buy ice cream on our return from the library. We hurried up the wooden pier, took the boardwalk around the ice cream shop, and stepped up onto the sidewalk.

CHAPTER SEVEN

At the Stratford Library

L arry headed straight to the card catalog to search for books about the Underground Railroad.

I followed at a leisurely pace, looking at everyone.

"Hello," said Mrs. Thomas, the large librarian. Busy with hot pink lipstick and short yellow ringlets of hair, her face made me nervous. When she said "hello," it sounded like an argument.

We liked the other librarian, Miss Penny. The one with red hair and a kind smile.

"Hello," I said, trying to sound uninterested in arguing.

I hurried on to join Larry. He stood at the card catalog, flipping through cards in one of the long wooden drawers. The rows and rows of cards overwhelmed me, but Larry loved them like old friends. Each index card held the name of a book or an author.

"What topic are you searching for?" I asked. "The Underground Railroad or Braggit clocks?"

Larry didn't answer. He was studying the card he had just picked up in his thin fingers.

"Here, write this down." He rattled off letters and numbers, and I wrote them in my notebook.

I followed Larry to the nonfiction section, trying to decide what the library smelled like. Paper, of course. Old books. Pencil lead. Carpet. Ink. But there was more than that. Perfume, especially if you got close to the yellow-haired librarian, Mrs. Thomas. Body odor, if you approached the old men dozing over magazines in the periodicals corner.

"Hello, boys."

"Hi, Miss Penny."

She had just emerged from between rows of books, pushing a metal cart.

"What are you looking for today, Larry? It looks like you're on a mission."

"I want more books about the Underground Railroad." Larry pointed to the numbers written on my notebook. "Do you know of any good ones?"

Miss Penny smiled again and nodded in the direction we had been heading. "You are going the right way." Then she stopped and frowned. "You know, Larry, you are an excellent reader, so it makes sense to come to the adult nonfiction. But I can tell you if you check the children's nonfiction, you might find some books with splendid pictures."

"That's a good idea," Larry said. "I'll do that. What about…
what's that clock name, Gary?"

I pulled my notebook out of my pocket and showed Miss
Penny.

"Hmm…" she said. "I don't know that name. Let's check the
encyclopedia, shall we?"

Larry and I followed her to the *World Book Encyclopedia*. She
grabbed the B volume and handed it to Larry, who searched the
B-R-A-G section.

"Not there," he said.

"Is this the name of a person?" Penny studied the letters in
my notebook from inside her cloud of wispy red hair.

"I think it's the name of a clock." I looked at Larry. "Although it might be named after a person."

"Ah. Do you know if this is the correct spelling? That sounds
like the way someone might try to pronounce a French name."

Miss Penny is so smart it's not funny.

"Yes, the spelling could be wrong." My spine tingled with
interest.

"Try an *e* instead of an *a*," she said. "B-R-E-G."

Larry flipped a few pages farther. "B-R-E-G—I found it."

"Great!" Penny whispered, reminding Larry to turn down
the volume of his voice. Penny doesn't even snap at us when we
are noisy. She just sets a good example.

"Is it a clock or a person?" I leaned over to see the entry.

"Person, Abraham-Louis." Larry's finger traced the small
print. "That antique dealer spelled it totally wrong. Ready?"

I grabbed my notebook and wrote as Larry announced the letters.

"B-R-E-G-U-E-T. Pronounced *bruh-GAY* with no *t* sound. He was the leading French hor—hor—"

"Horologist," Penny said. "It means a person who makes clocks and watches."

"Horologist of his time," Larry continued, "known for the profusion of his inventions and the exactitude of their execution."

"Wow." Penny smiled at Larry's fine pronunciation of the big words. "Too bad the writer had to use all those words instead of saying he invented many things and did everything carefully."

"Oh," I said. "So that's what that means."

She smiled. "Now if you like, while you boys check out the Underground Railroad, I'll see if we have any books about your new friend Breguet. That tiny encyclopedia article isn't very helpful."

"Speaking of clocks," I said, "could I find a book about Big Ben?"

"I'll check that too." She moved away with the metal cart.

In the adult section, Larry compared two books. I picked up a book and flipped through it. Then I started thinking about the smell again.

"I think this library smells worse each time we come here, don't you?" I asked Larry. "I didn't think about it earlier, but what a foul odor."

Larry glanced up from the books. But instead of looking at me, I saw his eyes flash up and past my shoulder, behind and above me. I whirled.

Raspy!

Oops. Wouldn't Mom snap if she knew I had talked about Raspy's smell again. But she would be glad to know Raspy had not died in the basement of Number Ten.

Raspy's white-yellow hair and chin stubble stood around his head like a rowdy field of wheat. His ever-present battered cap sat on his head like a second skull. As always, he hunched forward, a slight smile revealing tobacco-stained teeth and spaces where there were no teeth. His green cotton shirt hung around him, smudged and torn.

"You want to know about the Underground Railroad?" Raspy asked.

If you could hear him, you would know why his nickname was Raspy. His voice makes Larry's voice sound like a trumpet.

"Yes." Larry spoke quietly, as if to say that he did want to learn, but not if it meant a lesson from Raspy.

"Well, let me tell you a secret." Raspy held up a finger, pointing it toward us. "There was Underground Railroad right here in THIS TOWN. In THIS TOWN, back in them days."

When he spoke, a wave of onion breath hit me. I tried to back up slightly, but Larry wouldn't budge. I rested my wooden foot on his foot just to give him the idea, and he still wouldn't move an inch.

"Really?" Larry asked. "That's interesting."

I exhaled in frustration. Larry was playing along with Raspy, and now we would have an endless conversation. And Larry was not the one trapped beneath the man's stubbly chin.

"Tunnels!" Raspy sent a shower of spit out at me along with the letter t. "There is tunnels between some houses in this town. Down by the river."

"Really?" Larry dropped the books to his side and inched around me. I backed up a step, relieved. But Larry wasn't just talking with Raspy to be nice. He really wanted to know.

"Which houses?" Larry asked. "We live by the river. Do you think ours used to have a tunnel?"

"Probably still does," Raspy hissed, delighted at Larry's interest. "Probably still does."

This is getting ridiculous, I thought. Raspy would pump Larry full of myths. I decided it was time for the older brother to intervene.

"Have you ever seen one of these tunnels, Raspy?" I asked.

Raspy narrowed his eyes, as if he didn't quite like the older brother.

"I seen tunnels in this town."

"But not on our street."

"I seen tunnels." He pointed a finger right at me.

Yeah, yeah, I thought.

But Larry's blue eyes shone like stars in his thin face.

"Thanks, Raspy!" he said. "I'll check it out."

CHAPTER EIGHT

What the Police Found

Terry clunked the bowl of spaghetti and meatballs onto the table in front of me. I dished out a huge helping, despite the ice cream cones Larry and I had eaten only an hour before. I felt I would need extra calories just to manage all the thoughts swirling through my head. Larry shivered with excitement about Raspy's tunnel stories. He wanted to tell Terry about it after we were all safely in our room upstairs. Mom didn't need more worries, Larry told me, so the best way to show love was to keep Raspy's words a secret.

The words building up in my mouth distracted me from the tangled pasta and the spicy aroma of meat. "Mom? Aren't you going to talk to Dad about calling the police?"

There are a few rules in our house.

1. If our parents want to discuss something private, they send us outside.
2. If they disagree about something, it's private.
3. We three boys can give our opinions, but we have to do what our parents decide in the end.

So I wasn't sure we would get to hear the discussion about the odor next door.

"What now?" Dad didn't look in the mood for another police story. Terry had told him about Officer Jackson banning us from the street.

Amid bowls of green beans, applesauce, and spaghetti, a candle burned in a metal holder. Mom loved candles, because they made the house smell so good. Also, according to Mom, watching a quiet fire made a person smarter.

"Well, it's probably nothing." Mom shook Parmesan cheese onto her pasta. Mom isn't Italian at all. Her yellow hair and blue eyes are about as un-Italian as you can get. But she still cooks lasagna, pizza, and other Italian dishes. She met Dad when she was working in an Italian bakery and cafe.

Mom told Dad about the smell.

"We could go down there and look first." Terry adjusted a loose flap on one bandage. The bruise around his right eye had darkened to a deeper shade. "And then if it's something suspicious, we can call the police."

Dad chewed through three meatballs before speaking. I watched his fingers, holding the fork, still black with mechanic's grease that refused to come out with one washing.

"I think you're right, Bella," he said. "It's not our place to go into someone else's house. And there is something strange…"

He let his sentence die off into a shrug, kind of like a boat motor running out of gas. But a second later, he restarted his motor.

"You know, I wonder if we could get Harold to cut some shrubbery around that house. And those dead trees. I'll see if I can find out who bought the house. By the way, boys, Tina called me this morning and said she wants to go on a trip to visit her son. There's a German holiday she missed. She wants you boys to feed her dog while she's gone."

"You have got to be kidding." Terry let his fist fall on the table, shaking the candle flame. "What if we don't *vant* to?"

Larry and I snickered into our spaghetti, trying to muffle our humor. Tina often turned the *w* sound into the *v* sound, and Terry's rendition struck true.

"We have to do many things in life even though we don't want to," Mom said. "Also, it will give you a splendid chance to practice the first fruit of the Spirit."

"How are we supposed to love someone who calls the police on us?" Terry dug his fork into his spaghetti. "And then asks us for help the same day?"

Dad put down his fork and reached to the buffet behind him. He kept his Bible there for our morning devotional time.

"Look up Matthew chapter 5." He handed it down the table to Terry.

"Yeah, I know about loving your enemies." Terry took the book and sighed.

"It didn't really sound like it," Mom said.

I suppose having parents who agree with each other is a sign that you have a great family. But it's also a sign that you don't get anywhere when you try to argue.

"Maybe she will pay us a lot," Terry said. "Didn't you say she is rich?"

Dad shrugged. "Herbert owned a German clock company for many years, so she probably is wealthy. But if she is, no banker knows it."

"Why not?" Larry asked.

"Soon after we first moved here, when Herbert was still alive, one of his favorite employees robbed him of thousands of dollars. He distrusted banks before, but he got suspicious of everyone after that." Dad picked up the bread on his plate and took a bite.

"Did they ever catch the robber?" Terry asked.

Dad nodded. "I think he went to prison. But they still couldn't relax. Herbert put locks on all their windows and extra deadbolts on all the doors. Bella, this garlic bread. Excellent."

"So maybe she has treasure in there?" Larry scraped his plate clean of tomato sauce. "She should at least have plenty of money to pay us for feeding her dog."

"She has plenty of money because she saves everything and doesn't overpay the boys who feed her dog." Dad grinned at us.

We groaned.

Mom passed the garlic bread basket again.

"I told her you would be over tomorrow night for instructions." Dad picked out another piece of bread. "You can all three go the first time."

Well, that was that.

We couldn't do bicycle jump experiments in the street. And we had to feed a grouchy old lady's dog.

"So let's make our fruit of the spirit report for the day." Mom picked up her poster board chart with the word *love* written above the first of nine columns. "Did anyone see a person showing love?"

"Not Tina," Terry said.

Mom just smiled and didn't move her pen an inch.

"Oh, I know." Terry waved his fork, sending a dot of spaghetti sauce onto the poster board. "Harold. He talked to me for fifteen minutes about the boat races he's been in."

"Okay!" Mom jotted down the details. *Harold talked with Terry about boating.*

Dad opened his mouth and looked as close to speaking as a person can be without letting a word loose. Instead, he took a bite of garlic bread.

"Oh, I've got one too," Larry said. "Miss Penny at the library. She offered to help me find things even though I hadn't asked."

"She helped me too." I spooned up a pool of spaghetti sauce. "With a Big Ben book."

"Great job, everyone." Mom's pen scratched on the poster board. "Excellent. Did anyone think of a symbol for love? What is love like?"

"It's not like calling the police." Terry reached for more garlic bread, pleased with his thought.

All four of us burst out laughing.

"It's not like exposing teenagers to bad habits." Dad set down his spoon and fork and leaned back in his chair.

"What do you mean?" Mom asked.

Dad motioned with his hand. "I'll tell you later."

See what I mean? Our parents are so secretive sometimes.

"Love is like the North Star," Larry said. "It showed people where to go."

It took a moment of silence to absorb this bit of wisdom.

"The North Star." Mom forked her last bite of spaghetti, twirling it thoughtfully. "It shows people where to go. And, it always stays the same."

"And," Dad added, "the darker it gets outside, the brighter stars get."

"Excellent. We can keep thinking of ideas," Mom said. "Now everyone can have a cookie."

Terry dived for the cookie cupboard and pulled out the Tupperware cookie box.

Mom declined the cookies and reached for the phone book. On the inside front cover, she found the number for the police department.

Fifteen minutes after Mom's phone call, the same officer who ordered us off the street knocked on our door. He had three other officers with him.

"Officer Jackson," he said. "Hello again, ma'am." He even winked at us. "We are here to take a look next door."

The three of us and Dad sat out on our porch among Mom's pots of geraniums. Mom loves flowers as much as candles. This year, she filled the porch pots with deep red geraniums.

The front porch faced east, so the house sheltered us from the setting sun. The stench from the basement oozed up to the porch, making me want to gag.

I tried to imagine moving away from this comfortable porch. From the river behind our house. From Dad's boat motor shop. From the library. From our favorite maple tree in the back yard. From our bedroom, with its window looking out over the river. From the *London*.

Terry and Larry leaned over the porch railing facing the abandoned house. I sat in a wicker porch chair behind a pot of geraniums, resting my good leg on another chair.

"They're going to force entry." Terry leaned even farther over the rail, his bandages pointing toward Number Ten.

Crash! The police broke into Number Ten. We heard their footsteps thudding on the floorboards. Soon voices wafted through the broken window. In five minutes, they were back. Two of them wore gloves and held something between them on an open newspaper. As they flipped the object into a black trash bag, one of the outer pages of newspaper fluttered onto the porch.

"Dead cat," Officer Jackson called.

"One less cat in the world, at least." Terry had fought with cats twice. Both times, he had ended up with bandages.

"I thought we were going to have a mystery on our hands." Larry sighed. "Just a cat."

"I'm relieved we don't have a mystery on our hands," Dad said. "And your mother will be too."

"How long ago did you say you noticed occupants in this house?" Officer Jackson looked up at us.

The other officers fastened a new lock to the door.

"My wife saw people entering a week ago."

"Okay. Well, let us know if you see any more suspicious activity." The officers climbed into their cars.

"Thanks for coming out," Dad called after them. He turned and went into the house. He usually ended the day in his recliner, feet up, reading the newspaper and discussing pieces of it with Mom.

Larry turned to go after him. "I want to go read those books I got."

"Wait." I pointed toward Number Ten. "There's something else here for us to read."

"Are you crazy?" Terry raised his eyebrows, then winced. "I thought I was the one with brain damage. Where are you seeing something out here to read?"

I walked down the steps of our porch. Stepping over the yellow marigold row, I hurried over to the abandoned house. On the porch, I snatched up the newspaper page that had fluttered down.

"Aha!" Startled at my noise, I glanced at the open windows. If I wasn't careful, Mom and Dad would hear everything I said. Terry and Larry started toward me, down the steps. But I waved them toward the back of the house.

"Race you to the maple tree!"

CHAPTER NINE

What the Police Did Not Find

It was crazy for me to call the race, since I have the wooden leg. But I had a head start. We all collapsed together around the trunk of our favorite tree.

The maple tree has several attractive features.

1. Its branches are low and easy to climb.
2. It's tall, so it makes a great shady place during the day.
3. One of its branches curves past the porch roof under our bedroom window.

Why does it matter that the branch goes right past our window? Well, occasionally, it's easier to leave the house by stepping out of our bedroom window onto the back porch roof.

From the roof, we jump onto the maple tree, and from there to the ground.

"Get up." I pushed them ahead of me. "Let me show you something." We climbed into the tree. Immense clouds had piled up in the west, but the sun still shone down hot. It filtered through the green maple leaves, turning the leaves into sparkling jewels.

"Boat coming." Larry had the best ears. Seconds later, a motorboat shot through an arch of the Lexington bridge, leaving a wake that turned to gold in the sun.

"That's Harold." Terry waved a green branch wildly, but Harold looked straight ahead.

"Hopefully we can meet him sometime." Larry turned back to me. "But come on, Gary. What did you find?"

"This." I held the page up in front of them.

"Mayor Rules..." Larry read the headline.

"No, look at the date."

Terry narrowed his eyes and then winced again as a bandage stretched taut. "Monday, June 1, 1987. So?"

"That was four days ago." Larry said. "This week."

"Exactly." I let the page fall. It caught on a limb, then fluttered to the ground.

"Then it's been less than a week since someone has been in that house." Terry's eyes widened and his curls seemed to rise higher. "Someone must be sneaking in there when we aren't watching."

Larry frowned. "That newspaper came from the police."

"Maybe, but I don't think so." I shook my head. "They had nothing with them when they went down. I think the cat died on the newspaper since Monday. Or it died awhile ago and someone wrapped it in this paper hoping it wouldn't smell."

"Why wouldn't they just take it out?" Larry asked.

But I had remembered something else.

"Raspy! Larry, tell Terry what happened this afternoon at the library."

Larry frowned. He didn't like me linking suspicious activity next door to his splendid story from Raspy. Just at that moment, Mom opened the laundry room window right beneath the tree.

"Boys, come in and get ready for bed."

"Okay." Larry slid down the tree. "Hurry, Terry, and I'll tell you upstairs."

From his top bunk, Larry finally got to share about his conversation with Raspy.

We were all freshly bathed and dressed in our rumpled pajamas. It was still viciously hot, but the water had revived me. My wooden leg was finally off, resting in a corner of the room. I rubbed my stump. For those of you who have two legs, you do not know how good it feels to get a wooden leg off. The cool bed sheets soothed my stump.

As Larry talked, I lay on my back on the bottom bunk, my eyes wandering out the open window to where the clouds piled higher and higher like giant scoops of ice cream. The sun had dropped behind them and a hazy gloom covered the world. There would be no more golden glint on the river tonight.

In his single bed across from our bunks, Terry lay amid a chaos of stuff. Terry's corner of the room contained as many random items as Larry's and mine put together. Even if you counted my wooden leg.

Terry loved to build things, and he had a constant procession of models littering his dresser and bed.

1. Wooden car and train models.
2. Plastic truck models.
3. Small tubes of glue and pots of paint.
4. Train tracks.
5. Page after page of rope sketches.

Terry loves ropes. He rigged four lengths of rope from the curtain rod to his four bed posts. He ties different knots in the ropes, and sketches them on real drawing paper he bought with his wage from working at Dad's shop. Larry and I get a small allowance for mowing the lawn and helping Mom, but Terry makes more than we do.

I had practically tuned Larry out when Terry let out a re-sounding yell. "Waaa-hoo! An adventure."

"Shhhhhhh!" Larry said from above. "I didn't tell Mom. She would just worry."

Sure enough. "Everything all right up there?" Dad's voice from the bottom of the stairs.

"Yes."

"Sorry!"

"Now what's the adventure?" I turned to Terry. "Surely you don't believe Raspy's story? I mean, I believe he's sneaking around causing trouble. But tunnels?"

Terry sat up with a jolt, launching a wooden car onto the carpet. "Gary, don't you get it? Raspy could be down in Number Ten now, and that's where he found the tunnel. What if there's a tunnel into our basement? Raspy could break in."

I still didn't really believe that Raspy knew anything about tunnels. But Terry's enthusiasm infected me.

"Well, what do you want to do about it?" I sat up, swinging my good leg over the edge of the bed. My toes knocked my Rubik's cube to the floor. Now, my bed looks nothing like Terry's. But I have a few things scattered here and there. I often fall asleep with the Rubik's cube beside me, because I still haven't figured it out. Larry falls asleep with a book. I'm sure he has his new library books up there now.

"Listen guys." Terry leaned forward, hair wild, elbows on knees. "We wait until it's a little darker and then we check out the basement."

Larry swung out of the top bunk. This was getting serious. We all had to be on the same level.

"Wait." I frowned. "Our basement or the Number Ten basement?"

"Number Ten, of course." Terry ran his fingers up one of his ropes. "We've been in our basement all our lives and have seen nothing."

"I need my notebook for this." I flipped to a blank page. "Hang on."

Possibilities:

1. Raspy was lying and there are no tunnels.
2. Raspy was telling the truth and there are tunnels.

"We know that already." Terry chose a piece of rope from beside his bed. "Write something useful, will you? Make a list of what we should take with us. Larry, your flashlight."

"How are we going to keep from cutting ourselves on the broken glass?" Larry asked. "Mom picked up the pieces in the grass, but there are still shards in the window."

Terry grabbed the blanket off his bed and pulled. "Easy." A shower of wooden train tracks and cars rained through our room. Larry and I groaned.

"We are not picking up your junk," Larry snapped.

Larry is usually pretty relaxed. I wondered if he was getting nervous.

"Don't take your good blanket." I shook my head at Terry. "Let's get a rag. One that Mom uses to clean the bathroom. And I'm going to have to put my leg back on." I sighed.

"And we need a rope." Terry stepped into the hall for a rag.

"I'll untie one from my bedposts."

"Wait." My eyes darted to Larry's.

Terry stopped short. Larry stared back at me. "Where's that map, Larry?" My pulse pounded. "Could the map that Benjamin gave us show tunnels between the houses?"

"Ah!" Larry ran out of the room, nearly colliding with Terry.

"Where is he going?" Terry's hair stood on end like a forest of question marks above his wounds.

In two seconds, Larry was back with the pants he had been wearing. His thin hands darted into the pockets. "Here it is. Can't believe I forgot it."

We sat down on my lower bunk. Since he was the biggest, Terry sat in the middle with the map spread on his knees. Larry and I crowded in close on either side, trying to make sense of the boxes and squiggles.

"The boxes are houses." I pointed as I talked, catching Terry up from the conversation Larry and I had had earlier. "Have to be. And the squiggly line on the side is the river."

The first box had a short line leading off it with a circle at the end of that line. If our guesses were correct, that box was the house that had fallen down on the slope above Dad's garage.

The next box, our house, also had a short line and circle.

The next box, the Number Ten house, had a line connecting it to the next box, which would be Tina's house. At the same point where the line met Tina's house, another line led down to the river.

"Maybe Raspy is right," I said. "If there is a tunnel, this shows

71

that the tunnel goes from Number Ten to Tina's house."

"But what is that line off our house?" Larry asked. "If these are houses."

We shook our heads, puzzled.

"Wouldn't this be crazy?" My chin sank into my hands. "Maybe the Underground Railroad here really was underground."

"But wait." Terry stabbed a finger at the map. "How did we get this map from Red Hair and Raspy tells us about tunnels on the same day? That seems really strange. You don't think Red Hair works with Raspy, do you?"

We considered this.

"Maybe," I said. "It is odd that both things happened today."

"Benjamin is a professional," Larry said. "We don't even know that these lines are referring to tunnels. I think it is a coincidence we got this map and talked to Raspy on the same day."

"Okay." I shrugged. "The other thing is, I'm not sure that I trust Benjamin's map. Could be a made-up sketch."

"I believe Benjamin," Larry said.

"But someone could have given him a fake map." Terry reached for his piece of rope, and twisted it in his hands. "I agree with Gary. There's no point in putting stock in that map unless we find evidence it really means something. And that's what we're going to look for tonight."

CHAPTER TEN

A Nighttime Expedition

P reparations complete, we turned off our bedroom light and watched the sky through our window. It turned from greenish gray to gray-ish black. Finally, we could not even see the river.

"Let's go!" Terry climbed out of bed.

One by one, we slipped out of the window onto the back porch roof. We tiptoed to the tree. Catching the limb of the maple, we swung into our leafy friend. The tree swayed and dipped in a rising breeze. Larry held his light so I could see to get my footing.

In seconds, we were at the basement window, picking out shards of glass with our rag.

By the light of Larry's flashlight, Terry peered into the basement. "Nothing spooky," he said. "Just a normal basement. I'll hop in. Hang on to my rope."

Terry put his legs through the window first and slowly wriggled in. We had left the rag on the window frame to cushion the sharp edge. When he was mostly in, Terry grasped the rope with both hands. Larry and I hung onto the other end as Terry lowered himself down.

"All good!" His voice rose from the blackness. "Toss me the light."

With Terry and the light down in the basement, Larry and I followed easily. Neither of us needed the rope because Terry hauled us down.

"I feel like a firefighter." Larry flexed his biceps. "Except there's no fire."

I ignored his comment. I didn't like to think about firefighters now that I could never be one. Maybe his lungs would heal some day. But my leg would not.

"Looks kind of like a normal basement." Terry flashed the light on shelves crowded with boxes and jars, a rocking chair, stone walls, and a furnace.

"Bother." I stepped deeper into the basement. "I was hoping for a large wooden door with an iron ring on it."

Larry took his flashlight back from Terry. He had a terrible fear of small, dark places. Dad and Mom had given the flashlight for his birthday. They didn't say it, but I think they hoped the light would give Larry courage to explore some of those places that frightened him.

We followed the light as Larry searched the wall we had just descended, but nothing excited us.

"They call this a Michigan basement," Larry said. "A little like ours. Just rocks and cement and dirt."

"And a little remaining scent of rotting cat." I sniffed in disgust.

"Technically, there could be a tunnel behind these rock walls." Terry tapped the wall with his fist. "But if someone built the wall over the tunnel, it would take a bulldozer to dig it out."

We searched the wall toward the road. The old furnace blocked our view, but behind the furnace, the wall was solid cement. Nothing suspicious. Beside the furnace was a small wood-walled room with a doorway. Larry flashed the light into the room. The wood walls could be moved, but behind them, the stone wall of the basement ran unbroken. No doors or iron rings or any hint of a passage.

It was just a basement, thick with cobwebs, paint cans, tools, even an old exercise bike. In a corner lay a stuffed doll with yarn hair and button eyes. I wondered if the little girl who had been our neighbor had left it. We checked the third side. Nothing.

Larry swung his light to the fourth side toward the river.

"Whoa!" Terry stopped and held perfectly still.

We stared at a wooden door in the wall.

Larry and I joined Terry's perfect stillness. I can't speak for my brothers, but a cold, fizzy current crept up my back to the very roots of my hair.

Could it really be this simple? I thought. *A door to a tunnel right here in this house next door and we never knew it? And if so, what might we find behind that door?*

"I feel like Sherlock Holmes." Larry let out a long breath, like the far-off wavering of a train whistle. "See Gary, I told you we should listen to Raspy."

"Hang on, guys." The statue of Terry stepped off its base and became a real person again. Terry rushed to the wooden door. "It probably just goes to another room in the basement. Let's not get too worked up."

The door closed from the inside. Terry lifted the latch slowly, and the door opened toward us. A hinge whined. The bottom of the door scraped on the cement floor.

Our noses, eyes, and ears were just sending us signals that we were in the great outdoors, when a breath of wind hit us.

"Seriously, how dumb are we?" Terry smacked his head with his hand. "This is a door to the outside."

"But we never saw it from outside," Larry said.

Larry looked up, and his flashlight followed his eyes. The light reflected on a short flight of steps which ended with a plywood roof. The plywood did not completely cover the opening, allowing in wind and leaves and weeds. Two fat spiders glistened in the light.

"Oh… that's why we've never seen this. It's covered with plywood."

"Well, it's not like we spend time in this back yard, either," I said. "See, Larry. I told you we shouldn't listen to Raspy. Why would there be tunnels here?"

"I'm not a bit discouraged." Larry continued shining the light. "This would have been way too easy. I feel even more like

Sherlock Holmes now. Things were never as easy as an obvious door for him."

Through the long nights of winter, Larry often read to us out loud from the British detective story series.

"Well, aren't we a fine set." Terry shook his head, casting weird shadows on the ceiling. "Terrified over a cellar door. Let's—"

Daylight lit up the gaps along the sides of the plywood. We all jumped. Every shrub and weed and spider appeared in full color. Just as quickly, the world went black again. A boom of thunder shook the house.

"Speaking of being terrified." Terry laughed shakily, slamming the door shut.

A blast of wind shook the plywood and even the basement door. Rain pattered against the wood.

"Oh, man," Larry groaned. "We're going to get wet going back to the house."

"Let's wait just a moment." I headed back toward the wooden room, the rocking chair, and the cluttered shelves. To our right, wooden steps led to the first floor of the house. "We have to get back in through the tree, you know. That's not exactly safe in a lightning storm."

"Didn't think about that." Terry smacked his head with his hand again. "We should have brought a key. Mom and Dad are probably in bed, anyway."

A guilty silence filled the air.

1. We were smart enough to know we have great parents who actually care about us.
2. We felt a little guilty about leaving the house and entering a neighbor's house without telling them.
3. We preferred to avoid the topic for fear one of us would say these things.

"Hopefully Mom and Dad are not in our room checking to make sure we are doing okay with the storm." Larry shifted, his bare feet scuffing in the basement scum. We knew it was stupidity that none of us had shoes. But our shoes were downstairs, so we had come barefoot. The only foot that had a sock on it was my wooden one.

"Okay. Let's make use of our time and discuss the possibilities. Shine the light, Larry, and let's find stuff to sit on." I sank into the rocking chair. Terry found a five-gallon paint bucket. Larry fit on the side of a flimsy wooden crate stained with dark splotches, as if it had once held rotting fruit. Above us, whenever the light played that way, the joists of the first floor cast weird geometric shadows, scoring the lighter feathery shadows of spiderwebs. I thought I saw another fat-bodied spider as well, but I tried not to look.

"Don't suppose there are snakes down here?" Terry drew his feet off the floor.

Terry can meet any disaster, but he's terrified of snakes.

"Hard to say," Larry said. "It might serve us right for sneaking out if we get bitten by snakes."

"Oh, come on, Larry!" I was sure Terry rolled his eyes, but I couldn't see them. "Dad and Mom don't care if we do fun stuff. They just don't want us to bother them."

I opened my notebook to a blank page and clicked on my pen. The pen sounded like a gunshot in the silent basement with nothing but the noise of rain on the wooden door and the whispers of our own consciences.

"So." I slanted my notebook to catch the most light. "What are our conclusions from tonight's field trip?"

All I could see of Terry was a blurry shadow topped with frizzled hair. He had drawn his feet up onto the bucket, and sat perched like a contorted owl on a pole.

"I'm not convinced the tunnel thing is false." Larry tapped his fingers on his wooden seat, trying to keep his light on my paper with the other hand. "I want to go investigate our own basement tomorrow in the daylight and look for patches in the stone."

I scribbled "Larry" and "not convinced" on the paper.

"I don't give any weight to Raspy or anything he says." I leaned back in the rocker, knocking over something that sounded like glass but didn't break. "Yeah, maybe he's seen one tunnel down the river somewhere, but there are a ton of houses on this river. And we have no proof he's ever been in this house."

At that exact moment, something that wasn't thunder banged upstairs. We all jumped. Again.

"What was that?" Terry stiffened on the bucket.

"It sounded like a door slamming." Larry instinctively shielded the light with his hand.

We all stood, careful to avoid bumping into anything. Terry motioned to us to follow him. Larry snapped off the flashlight. As we tiptoed after him, we heard footsteps crossing the floor above us. We didn't need to communicate the obvious.

1. The noises were not made by a cat.
2. A person was in the house above us.
3. We didn't want to meet that person here on a dark, rainy night.

We crouched under the window we had come through. Should we make a dash out the window? Or stay completely quiet and hope the footsteps would go away? We didn't have to decide, because the door above the basement steps squeaked open. The beam of a flashlight wavered through. Feet hit the top step.

We clutched at each other. My hand dug into Terry's forearm. Larry's thin hand cinched a death grip around my arm. Terry had both of us by a shoulder, as if he considered hurling us through the window.

The feet shuffled down, lower and lower, in a circle of light. At the bottom of the stairs, the light swung toward the rocking chair. The man—for we were sure it was a man, although we couldn't see well—headed to the place we had been sitting moments before. He sat down in my seat, the rocking chair, and set the flashlight on the five-gallon pail Terry had been sitting on. In his other hand, he held a white paper bag from a fast-food restaurant, which he opened. He pulled out a paper-wrapped sandwich, his hands reflecting white in the light. He put his feet on the crate where Larry had been sitting moments before.

He paused, pulling a long something from a holster at his side. A line of silver flashed in the darkness. *A knife!*

Then he leaned over the sandwich and took a bite. As he did so, his head came into the light and I saw a tight, smudged cap, uneven stubble, and gaps where teeth should have been.

Raspy!

We were trapped in an abandoned basement with Raspy and a long knife.

CHAPTER ELEVEN

A New Assignment

Terry's fingers tightened on my shoulder as I stared through the darkness at Raspy. The aroma of cheeseburger mingled with body odor. The big question was, would Raspy shine his light our way? Or would there be another flash of lightning? However, I was pretty sure I knew what Terry's fingers meant, biting into my shoulder: *Don't move.*

Lightning. The basement lit up, then darkened. Raspy still munched, elbows on knees, not looking up. He finished the sandwich, crumpled the paper into a ball, and tossed it under the shelves behind him. Then he pulled a well-worn blanket out of a box in the darkness. He folded it into a pillow, which he placed behind his head, propped his feet on the wooden crate, and snapped off the light.

Several thoughts flooded me at once.

1. Hurray! The light is gone.
2. Oh, no. We can't see him anymore.
3. Oh, no. With the light gone, his eyes will adjust to the dark and he may see us.

We waited.

Standing still is actually hard work. I never realized this before. My good leg ached. My wooden leg angled crookedly and pinched my skin. The musty basement tickled my nose. I had to sneeze.

Just then, Terry relaxed his grip. Across the basement, a rhythmic purring sound came from the rocking chair. Raspy was sleeping.

"Larry first." Terry turned toward the window. Together we raised Larry up. Rain still poured down and streamed in the cement window well, but we didn't care. All we wanted was to escape.

Larry out. Rope handed up to Larry. Terry lifting me. Scrambling through window. Both of us holding the rope. Terry through window.

"Yee-haw! We made it." Terry took off like a bolt of lightning for the maple tree.

Larry and I blew out a breath of relief and followed. The lightning and thunder were distant now. We just wanted to be warm and dry in our rooms.

We slipped and slid on the bark of the maple and tiptoed nervously across the porch roof. But at last we were peeling off our wet clothes.

"11:40." Terry threw his damp shirt across the room. "I didn't think we were gone that long."

"We've got to wash our feet." Larry pointed at the mud splatters on his own feet.

Mom had a sharp eye for dirt, especially on bed sheets. Thankfully, Terry had failed to hang his towel in the bathroom, so we used the towel to clean our feet.

I removed my wooden leg again and dived into bed. *Delightful.* The storm had washed the heat from the air. A cool breeze came through the open window. Rain had come in too, but it had only dampened my bedding and a bit of carpet. It would dry.

Now that we were safe and still alive, we discussed the events of our escapade. It was Saturday the next day. The beginning of the weekend meant we could sleep in.

"What do you think he's doing down there?" Larry stuck his head over the edge of his bunk. "He looks kind of like John the Baptist eating in the wilderness."

"Pretty sure he's not on the same mission as John the Baptist," Terry said.

"Well, neither are we." Larry threw out an arm in protest. "Sneaking out without permission."

"Now, look here." Terry finished cleaning his feet and pitched the towel on the floor amid the supplies he had scattered earlier. "Let's just give ourselves a week to investigate. Mom and Dad never told us we couldn't check things out after dark, so we're not disobeying them. And we will not get killed in one week."

"I can think of a lot of ways to die in one week," Larry said.

Terry picked up his pillow and hurled it toward the top bunk. Larry ducked into bed and the pillow thumped against the wall behind him.

"Well, we don't even need a week to finish this investigation." I curled deeper into the clean sheets. "If we get a good chance to go downstairs, we can check our own basement for clues tomorrow. If we find nothing, we drop it. Then we assume the map is fake, and Raspy was lying."

"Shouldn't we tell someone that Raspy is living over there?" Larry's voice fell from the top bunk.

Sometimes things would just flow better if Larry didn't have such a conscience.

"Um… there's an obvious problem with that." Terry's words tumbled out, mixed with sarcasm.

"Yeah," Larry said. "I can only imagine Mom's first question."

"Yes, she'll ask how we know Raspy is living there," I said.

"Just a week." Terry snapped off the light. "We'll let them know about our investigation in a week, and they'll be glad we didn't worry them by saying something sooner."

When the three of us straggled downstairs at 9:00 the next morning, Dad was already out. Mom turned the burner on the stove to heat the griddle for another run of pancakes.

"Where's Dad?" I dropped into my chair, eager to get on any topic that didn't involve last night.

"Tina called this morning." Mom poured oil on the griddle and spread it with a turner. "She had a tree fall in the storm last night."

"On her house?" I poured myself a glass of milk and passed the jug to Terry. Larry preferred orange juice.

"No, but it took out a section of her fence. Dad went to look at it, but I think he's going to suggest she call Harold."

"Oh, right." Terry perked up. His face looked worse than it had yesterday. Dark purple bruising stained his right eye. "Harold's a tree trimmer. Maybe if we're over there feeding the dog while he's cutting up trees, he'll give us a ride on his boat."

"Trees can be dangerous." Mom poured white, foamy pancake batter onto the glistening hot griddle. "I don't want you boys sneaking around while he's doing that."

We stared at our drinks. On the scale of danger, trees sounded like blades of grass to us after last night's adventure.

Bubbles formed on the edges of the pancakes. Mom expertly tested one with her turner. Light brown pancake peeked out at me, but it didn't pass Mom's inspection yet.

"What are we doing today?" Larry sipped his juice.

Mom's words hit us like sunrise after a dark night.

"I'd like you three to work on cleaning the basement." She tested another pancake, then began flipping. The delicious, sweet-oily smell of sizzling pancakes entranced us almost as much as the instructions to work in the one place we wanted to investigate. "I know it's not a fun job, but work hard for an hour or two and you should be done. I might need you in the garden a little, but you will still have time to take your boat out before supper."

Saturdays at our house meant the best food in the world. Pancakes for breakfast. Popcorn and apples and cheese for lunch. And then, the highlight of the week for supper: Mom's homemade pizza.

"Sure, we can clean the basement," Terry said expansively. I almost choked, hoping he wasn't sounding *too* eager. Mom opened her mouth as if to say something, but the pancakes were ready, so she served us three each.

"Terry, you can bless the food." She took the griddle to the sink.

"God, thank you for these pancakes." Terry cleared his throat dramatically. "And thank you for the health and strength to clean the basement today."

This was too much. Larry and I both burst out laughing.

"Amen." Terry said, annoyed. "Stop laughing at my prayer, will you?"

Mom shook her head. "You must have gotten a good rest, Terry."

I sympathized with her confusion. Terry was not known for thanking God for cleaning jobs. Again, my conscience pricked me. Should we tell Mom?

But she hadn't asked. And like Terry said, she would worry less this way. We slathered our pancakes with butter and poured on warm maple syrup.

Mmm… there is simply nothing as great as a warm fluffy pancake dripping with butter and syrup. Well, besides Mom's pizza.

CHAPTER TWELVE

A Clue and a Chore

I n the basement, Mom set us to work. She gave Terry the vacuum cleaner and told him to suck up every spider and spiderweb. She assigned the paint room to Larry, and the extra pantry to me.

"Everything comes off the shelves." She pulled off a glass jar and carried it to the top of the freezer. "Then let Terry vacuum the shelves. Then you wash them and put everything back as you found it. Or better."

Like Larry, Mom preferred things in order. Possibly it was those blue eyes, able to spot every flaw.

With Mom upstairs, we had to work diligently on our assigned tasks before we could do any sleuthing. But as I unloaded glass jars of applesauce and tin cans of baked beans, my eyes wandered over the wall behind the wooden shelves. I studied the stones and mortar and tried to imagine a pattern covering a secret entrance. I picked out a large jar of pickles. Just as I turned to add them to the top of the chest freezer, something caught my eye.

What was it?

A piece of rock had fallen onto the shelf behind the pickle jar. A scattering of mortar dust and chips surrounded it. I picked up the rock. The wall was old, and mortar often fell from it. But I had never seen such a big rock work its way out. It was half the size of my head. I reached my fingers into the cavity it had slid from. It was under the wooden shelf, so I couldn't see well, and it took me a minute to understand what I was feeling.

Nothing.

There was nothing at the back of the cavity. No wall. Just space.

A chill of excitement shot through me. Of course, I couldn't reach my hand in far. But I should have hit something. I turned and dashed to the paint room.

"Larry, come look at this." As I hurried back, I motioned to Terry. He turned off the vacuum cleaner and joined us.

"A hole." I bent down and pointed under the shelf. "I can't feel anything in there. No wall."

Terry grabbed an old flashlight from Dad's work bench. "What are the odds this thing has batteries?"

"I've got my flashlight too." Larry pulled it out, but Terry flipped the switch on Dad's light, determined to see if it worked.

If we held our hands right in front of Terry's light, a dim white pool formed on our hands. Terry crouched low, put his head under the shelf, and held the light against the hole.

My eyes met Larry's over his arched back. We both shivered with anticipation.

"Hard to tell." Terry's voice rose like vapor from the tight space.

"Here, use mine." Larry held out his flashlight.

"Let me look." I took the light. "It's my discovery."

I crouched on my good leg, letting my wooden leg stick out behind me. I wedged my head under the shelf. It took me awhile to figure out how to hold Larry's flashlight so the light wouldn't just reflect off the mortar. Finally, I got it focused on the hole. Terry was right. There wasn't much to see.

I let my eyes relax, then tried again. I shut the right one and focused the left, holding my breath.

Suddenly, air rushed into my lungs. I saw rock wall. Not close to me, but at least four or five feet away.

I pulled myself out and straightened up. My voice shook. "It's a secret room. Or a tunnel. I'm sure of it. I saw rock wall five, six feet away."

"Raspy was right." Larry pushed his head under the shelf. "And Benjamin's map."

"We still don't know if that map is right." Terry frowned. He was probably irritated that I had seen something first.

"Yes, we do." Larry straightened up. "On that map, the second box–which could be our house- had a short line and circle coming off it, toward the river. That matches with this."

"Here's the problem." I held up a hand. "If the map is right, this is just a secret room that goes nowhere. Raspy said there were tunnels."

"Well, Raspy could still be right and the tunnels are somewhere else," Larry said. "The map shows tunnels between the next houses."

"Boys!" Mom's voice from the top of the stairs.

"Yeah?"

"Try to finish up quickly. I need your help in the garden."

"How does that garden always ruin our plans?" Terry muttered as he headed back to the vacuum cleaner.

"It doesn't." I sighed and picked up another pickle jar. "Yesterday it was Tina."

Dad called Tina's house an engineer's nightmare. A cube-like shape in the center made us realize it was a house. But every corner bulged with strange shapes, carved trim, or colored glass. Two chimneys pierced the sky like the horns of an exotic animal. The bronze owl on the front porch steps stared at the street, unblinking.

It was late afternoon by the time we headed toward her house, after a lot of work and a very short spin on the river.

Larry had read an article about Rottweilers once, and he told us what he remembered as we walked. Rottweilers were a German breed. Of course, Tina would have a German breed of dog. Germans called them "butcher's dogs" because they once pulled carts of butchered meat to market. He also informed us that male Rottweilers could be aggressive, especially if they were not used to being around people.

Past the wooden fence with the kayak tied to it. Past the bronze owl. Up onto the porch.

The old lady let us in. Up close, her white hair looked like cotton. Her nose bulged. Behind her, dozens of painted eyes stared at us out of a china cupboard. Apparently, Tina collected ceramic dolls.

"Come zis way." Tina marched down the hallway, opened a door, and slowly descended the basement steps, taking one step at a time.

"You must meashure very carefully." Tina's voice buzzed at us like a saw blade from above the dog food bag.

Mom had taught us that the German language had no *zh* sound as is found in English words like *measure* or *leisure*. Tina used the *sh* sound instead.

"Dog food in America cost too much." She shook dog food into a plastic cup.

We were standing at the bottom of Tina's basement stairs, in a cocoon of newsprint. Tina had wall-papered every wall with newspaper clippings. German words covered most of them. Along the south wall, the clippings were yellow and crumbling. Under this ancient decor, a huge dog box held the Rottweiler. An old green refrigerator sat nearby in the corner. On the next wall, close to the refrigerator, a tiny stuffed rocking chair and a two-shelf bookcase showed that Tina herself joined her pet down here. Knotted ropes and soft furry dog toys littered the linoleum floor.

"How much does dog food cost in Germany?" Terry asked.

I sank my elbow in his ribs.

"Remember what Mom said," Larry mouthed from behind Tina's back.

Just before we walked over to Tina's house, Mom had admonished us. "Don't forget about your fruit of the Spirit project. Tina needs love as much as anyone."

Now Tina replied in a no-nonsense tone, eyes boring into Terry. "Iss very cheap."

"Does the dog stay in his crate all day?" I hoped to steady the rocking conversation. I knew her dog ran in the back yard frequently because we could often hear him barking.

"No, no, only in big storm." Tina walked to the dog crate. "And when people come he not like. I leaf him out of crate, he bite you if he not like you." Her wrinkled face broke into a smile.

Our faces paled.

"Will he bite us when we feed him?" Larry asked thinly.

"I zink he will not bite you," Tina said. "He will be used to you. Come."

Tina slid the bolt back on the crate.

"Cum, Fritzie, good dog." She put her hands around his head, scratching behind his triangular black ears. His nose shone black and his rapid panting revealed a pink tongue. Brown fur outlined his muzzle and the tops of his eyes. His four feet and two patches on his chest were brown as well, but the rest of him was charcoal black. He stood on all fours, waiting to charge.

"Touch, touch," Tina said. We all scratched Fritz's ears. He sniffed us suspiciously, but did not growl or bark.

"I leaf him out now. He know you now. But I always feed him in crate. Iss goot."

"Okay." Terry wanted to regain ground with Tina. "So we feed him in the morning and in the evening? And do we let him—"

"No!" Tina's eyes lit like torches. "Not in zee morning. Only in zee evening. German dogs are so strong. You put him out in yard for walk morning and evening, but you only feed in evening.

"And one zing important." She shook her finger at us. *"Let no one else* come in my house. *No."*

We nodded.

CHAPTER THIRTEEN

I Write a Letter

Over pizza that night, Dad updated Mom on our progress with the fallen tree. After getting instructions about how to take care of Fritz, we had gone into the backyard to help Dad.

"We cut enough to fix her fence. That's what really matters, her being able to let her dog run free."

"Is Harold going to work on the rest of it?" Mom cut the homemade pizza into squares so we could all have a second piece.

"I called him earlier to see if he was available, and he was." Dad paused, with a piece of pizza halfway to his mouth. "I suggested she call him and left her the number. But she didn't seem interested in hiring someone she doesn't know."

"She doesn't like visitors," I said. "I'm surprised she's letting us take care of Fritz."

"She's not very loving." Terry picked up a fallen piece of pepperoni and popped it into his mouth.

"Well, I think the three of you were." Mom nodded toward the posterboard hanging on the fridge by a magnetic clip.

We all ate too much pizza, like we did every Saturday night. Mom had just the right ingredients in the sauce and just the right ratio of cheese to crust.

An hour later, Larry and I deadlocked in a game of chess. Both of us lay on the carpet. The wooden chess board that Dad crafted in high school lay between us. Over in the library on Mom's table, Terry puzzled over a complex Lego design, mumbling that he really must be missing a piece this time.

Dad read the newspaper on his recliner.

After putting away the dishes, Mom had disappeared to the room off the library, which she and Dad kept as an office.

"Checkmate!" Larry's voice burst with triumph.

"What? Are you sure?" I studied my options.

His bishop had moved only two squares, pinning down my king. I searched for a space to move to for safety. None.

I could only stare. "I can't believe I missed that. I saw your bishop, but I didn't see the queen in line."

"Well, it wasn't in line before." Larry pointed. "But you just moved your pawn out of the way for me."

"Oh, right."

We sent the pieces clattering into their bag.

"Gary, come here for a moment." Mom, calling from the office.

That was unusual. Had I gotten into trouble?

Mom sat in her office chair in front of a desk cluttered with food pantry fliers, coupons, and several books. In her hand, she held a folder.

"What?" I asked, dropping into Dad's office chair. His desk here was neater than Mom's, but his main desk at the shop was so cluttered you couldn't find the top.

"Why don't you write a letter to your surgeon?" She looked at me closely. "Ask him if you can talk to him."

The muscles in my neck tightened. I leaned back into the chair, trying to relax. "How would that help?"

"You do better with things you understand. You are a detective."

"Maybe." I wondered what Mom would think if she knew just how much of a detective I had been in the last two days.

Mom looked through medical papers in a folder.

"Can I see that?" I had never looked at it before.

"I was looking for something that would explain the cancer you had." Mom handed the folder to me. "But I can't find it. The surgeon would have the documents and could explain to you exactly what happened."

I pulled out the top sheet of paper. *Our patient today is a seven-year-old male presenting with an injury to the knee and a suspicious radiography report.*

Suspicious.

"Okay." I snapped the folder shut. "What do I say?"

"Just be honest. Say you were a patient six years ago and that you are wondering if you could talk to the surgeon. Maybe they won't let you… but it can't hurt to try."

"Hopefully I don't bite his head off."

"Hopefully not." Mom smiled. "Why don't you write up the letter tomorrow after church. I can look over it with you. Then we can mail it Monday. Or, if I can find a fax number, you could take it to the library and fax it."

Dear Dr. Jefferson.

It was a sleepy Sunday afternoon. Terry and Dad napped in the sitting room. Mom dozed between chapters of a book. Larry sat in the library, reading the book about clocks.

I had only a vague memory of Dr. Bruce Jefferson. Mostly, I remembered a black beard and a long, waving arm, as Dr. Jefferson explained things to my mom.

And I remembered the pain in my foot that night after my amputation. Only my foot wasn't there anymore.

Dr. Jefferson wasn't there through the night either. Only the nurse and Mom remained as I battled the pain.

The nurse rubbed and rubbed the blanket where my foot had been. Even though I knew it was ridiculous, it seemed to help.

Should I relive those painful memories by writing to Dr.

Jefferson? But I wanted to know. Had it been necessary, *really* necessary to cut my leg off?

When I was seven years old, you amputated my leg…

"Gary, listen to this." Larry came out to the kitchen where I worked on the table. "This Breguet clock maker, he made clocks for the French royal family. And he made a clock that could wind watches."

I looked up from my letter. He held the book open so I could see the picture. A small clock face peered at me from the center of a jeweled box standing on four small feet.

"See, at the top, you set the watch." Larry pointed. "And the watch winds on its own. He told his son that he had made a very important invention and that he shouldn't tell anyone about it. And that he thinks he will have the greatest fame and fortune because of it."

"Did he get his fame and fortune from making these clocks?"

"Uh… not sure yet." Larry took a chair beside me and continued to read silently. Whenever he found something especially fascinating, he read it to me out loud.

Apparently, Breguet worked so carefully and slowly that he never accomplished much. He only made twelve of the watch-winding clocks in his lifetime.

"Oh, this one is in Illinois." Larry pointed back to the picture. "A French prince ordered it in 1832 to decorate his apartment in Paris. Then the prince died in a freak carriage accident ten years later and the clock disappeared until this Mr. Daniels found it for a museum in Rockford, Illinois."

"Where did he find it?" I erased a mistake in my letter. I was almost done.

"In Paris," Larry said. From my project in the hospital, I knew this was the capital of France. "An antique dealer helped him find it. It was missing parts, but he fixed it."

Larry put down his book just as I signed my name: *Sincerely, Gary Fitzpatrick.* He looked at me with dreamy eyes.

"What if that antique dealer is right? There might be one of these clocks in our neighborhood."

I shrugged. "I thought you said it was in Illinois."

"Well, of course, that one is. But there are others."

"I doubt it. If he's that famous, they probably know where the others are."

"Yeah." Larry toyed with the corners of the book.

"I don't understand why Benjamin gave us that map." I folded my letter. "It says nothing about clocks on there."

"Let's find another clue tomorrow in the base—"

"Shhhh." I pointed to the sitting room.

He nodded.

It was almost more than we could do to wait until Monday to investigate the basement again. But wait we must if we were going to do it without disturbing Mom.

CHAPTER FOURTEEN

The Second Map

Monday afternoon, the three of us folded laundry with speed before unknown to humanity. Even Terry was home, since Dad had a light day at the shop. Mom was at work in the garden for a few hours, so we had the house to ourselves. Or, more importantly, the basement.

We stuffed the laundry in drawers and dashed down to the pantry shelves.

"That was the longest weekend I've ever lived," Terry said, rope in hand. "Finally!"

"We made it through without being murdered in our beds." I began unloading jars from the shelves. We would have to move them all again. "That counts for something. And it doesn't look like this hole has changed."

"It's about to, though." Larry cheered, flashlight in hand. "I feel like Hezekiah in the Bible building the underground aqueducts."

"That was Solomon," I said.

"It was Hezekiah."

Terry rolled his eyes. "Come on, you fighting children. Let's get these cans off, and fast. I'll run up to the garage and get some tools for taking the shelf apart."

Writing the letter to Dr. Jefferson had helped me immensely, and I was in a good mood. Somehow, just thinking someone important like him might listen made me feel much better. Mom had found the fax number for the doctor's office in Chicago, and I had boated it to the library myself.

By the time Terry returned with a hammer, nails, and a pry bar, Larry and I had cleared the shelves.

"Hey, these aren't built into the wall." Terry inspected the shelves, hammer in hand. "They are just sitting here."

"Could the shelves be as old as the secret room?" I pulled at the wooden uprights. "Maybe someone built them to cover it."

"I feel like Christopher Columbus." Larry's breath chopped his sentence short. "Look at this."

He was lying on the floor on his stomach, looking up at something joining the two sections of shelving. His mouth hung open.

"It's a hinge. And look there's one at the top. How did we not notice?"

"Impossible." Terry touched the metal hinge at the top of uprights, as if to see if it was real. "But there it is. That means we have been coming down to get stuff for Mom all these years, and we've never noticed it."

"With a hinge, we can just fold this section forward." I tapped the section of shelves that stood in the way of the hole in the wall.

"They are probably rusted." Terry pulled on the section, and nothing moved. "Larry, can you run for oil?"

We slathered the hinges with oil, but the shelves refused to budge.

"Let's just move the whole thing." Terry went to one end of the shelving and lifted.

Here, we had another surprise. Someone had bolted the shelves to the floor on that end. The bolt looked as rusty as the hinges. Finally, with Terry striking the hinges with a hammer and Larry and me pushing, we forced the unbolted half of the shelf unit forward, screaming on the rusted metal.

"Okay, quick." Terry took the pry bar to the rocks in the wall. Because the mortar had already crumbled, breaking the second rock free took us only fifteen minutes. The third came even faster. The fourth created a hole big enough for us to get through.

"Okay, here goes." Terry looked at us, grimy with dust and perspiration, wild with excitement.

"There might be snakes in there," I said.

Terry grimaced but hardened his face. "I'll take the risk."

Larry switched on his flashlight. His face paled. He hated tight spaces.

Terry, then me, then Larry. Into the secret room. We couldn't stand fully upright because the floor of the secret room was higher than the basement floor. With Larry's light, we saw crude lumber slats supporting the ceiling. Fortunately, no living spiders caught my eye.

The room was about six feet deep and six feet wide.

"Aw." Terry walked around the perimeter, ducking his head. "I was hoping there was a door or an entrance to a tunnel."

"Well, isn't this how the map showed it?" Larry shrugged. "The little circle on the map is this little room."

"Maybe," Terry said. "Still, I'm a little disappointed."

"Bottom line we still don't know if the map Benjamin gave us is trustworthy." I squinted around the dark space as my eyes adjusted "He could have just made it up."

"But this fits the map," Larry said.

"It does, but that could be chance. It doesn't mean those other lines are actually tunnels between the houses."

"I guess." Larry moved toward the entrance. "Well, this is getting too stuffy for me. I think I'll step back out. You can have my light."

"Not much here, I guess." I watched Larry wriggle out through the hole, debating if I should follow him.

"A great secret room, though." Terry flashed the light around the room. "We should put some chairs down here and keep secret documents in a safe."

"Do we have secret documents?"

"Minor issue." Terry waved away my objection. "You could make us some."

We were just turning to go when the light picked up a texture I hadn't noticed before.

"Hold it." I grabbed at the flashlight.

"What?"

"Give me that light. I saw something in that corner."

I stepped toward the corner, leaning down to see more closely. Yes, a pointed edge. Of something. I reached out two fingers, pinched the object and pulled it toward me. Terry reached in a long hand and grabbed the object. I held the flashlight to it.

In his hand, he held a cracked, dirt-caked leather bag.

"What is going on in there?" Larry looked in through the hole.

"Not sure." Terry moved toward him. "We got loot. Coming out to the light."

We scrambled out into the main part of the basement. In this improved lighting, the dirty bag showed a faint brown color.

"I feel like King Josiah in the Bible." Larry touched the bag, eyes full of awe. "When they discovered the old book of the Law in the Temple."

"Pretty sure this doesn't contain a book of the Law." Terry eased open the mouth of the leather bag. "Ugh, the leather and paper are so brittle I'm afraid I'll break it."

"Paper?" Larry's blue eyes expanded. "Here, let me try, my fingers are smaller than yours."

Larry slid his thin fingers into the bag. He couldn't see what he was doing. His eyes stared up at the ceiling as he concentrated.

"It's stuck." He grimaced. "I'm trying to separate it."

"We could cut the leather." Terry reached for his pocketknife.

"No," Larry said. "It might be a hundred years old. I think I've got it."

He slowly removed his hand. Between the ends of his fingers he held something thin and brown and several inches square. "Oh no, I broke off a piece."

I reached for the bag. "Let's turn it inside out."

"Nothing else in there, huh?" Terry said. "Not even one nugget of gold or an old coin?"

"Nope, nothing." I felt the bottom of the bag.

The cool air of the basement fell silent as we stared at the brittle note. Black stains covered it as if it had once been moldy. Someone had folded it in half.

"It's going to break when we open it." Larry eased on the two sides, but they stuck fast. "I wonder if we could soften it with water?"

"Let's go upstairs." I led the way to the stairway, holding the leather bag.

In the bathroom, we softened the old paper with a few drops of water. Using tweezers from the medicine cabinet, which Mom usually used to search for slivers of wood embedded in our feet or fingers, we pulled the pieces apart.

A hole remained where the piece had stuck to the inside of the bag. With the same technique, we loosened the chip from the inside.

With the tweezers, I took the chip and placed it in the empty space on the paper.

"Oh." I leaned in closer. "It's the same map."

Larry pushed me away. "Are you sure?"

I nodded. "It's just stained and torn. But look at that squiggly line. It's the river, just like the other map showed."

"Ah-ha!" Larry cheered, clapping his hands. "Do you believe Benjamin now? He didn't make up his map. It's a copy of an old map."

"I think I see letters on this one." Terry squinted his eyes. "Or words. What does it say?"

My eyes widened. "You're right. It's pencil markings."

"I can't believe I'm the one solving this," Terry said, after a hard look, "but I'm pretty sure it says YOU ARE HERE."

Again, Larry and I had to take turns sticking our heads over the paper, but we concluded Terry was right.

"It says YOU ARE HERE, in that little circle off our house," I said. "Which is exactly what we expected by looking at the other map. So the tunnel from Number Ten to Tina's house must be there too."

We stood in silence, astonished and delighted. We had our own genuine mystery to solve.

CHAPTER FIFTEEN

Feeding Fritz

Monday night before supper, we headed for Tina's house. I stuffed my notebook in my pocket. Larry's flashlight bulged from his pocket for some unknown reason. Terry carried a baseball bat, also for an unknown reason.

"Seriously, Terry." I pointed to the bat. "You cannot use that on Fritz."

"Gary, be quiet." Terry walked ahead along the curb, the hand with the bat extended to keep balance. He stepped down into the road. "Do you want to come out alive, or have Fritz come out alive?"

"Both."

"But if something bad happens, and that butcher cart beast lunges for your throat, you'll be glad I have this along." He strolled on ahead, swinging the bat.

He had a point.

We had passed the abandoned house, and I glanced back at it. A tangle of weeds obscured the basement windows on this side. Hidden tunnels swirled through my thoughts.

"When are we going to look for signs of the tunnels?" I asked. "And where?"

"Tomorrow." Terry threw the bat in the air and caught it. "And I say we start with a better look in Number Ten during daylight hours. Mom is going to work in the garden again. She won't mind."

"Yes, but I think she wants us to help weed," Larry said.

"Well, I'm not going to nominate you for a loving deed." Terry caught the bat again. "Why did you have to remind us?"

We walked past the steady eyes of the bronze owl and climbed up Tina's stone porch steps. Terry fitted the key into the lock and we went in. It felt odd to be walking into someone else's house when they weren't home. It felt even odder because it was Tina's house. A strange smell of sauerkraut mixed with cinnamon, plus a touch of laundry soap, rushed up our noses. Tina's china cabinet filled with porcelain dolls stared at us with their fixed, painted eyes. Above the cabinet, a cuckoo clock announced five o'clock.

We slipped out of our shoes and headed to the basement stairs.

Tina had left just that morning. She said she would leave Fritz in his kennel and we could let him out. This might endear him to us more easily. After that, we would let him roam the house freely as she did.

We clattered down the stairs.

"Do we let him outside first or feed him first?" Larry looked at Terry and I. None of us could remember.

"I say we let him run outside first." Terry headed for the crate.

Under the wall of newspaper words, the Rottweiler looked up at us wagging his tail.

"Nice," Larry said. "I think he knows we are going to let him out."

Terry lifted the latch and swung wide the wire mesh door. The dog bolted from his prison and sprinted up the carpeted stairway.

"No worries about getting bitten." I laughed, turning to watch him go. "He doesn't even care that we exist."

"He will when we break out the food," Terry said.

Fritz had beaten us to the back deck door off the dining room. He whined and pressed his nose to the glass. Terry whipped open the door, and Fritz raced across the deck and into the lawn, barking joyfully.

What a beautiful night! Friday's storm had wiped the stickiness from the air. The fallen fir tree stretched across the yard, leaving a space between the two other fir trees facing south toward Number Ten. The line of three fir trees on the north side of Tina's back yard stood tall and strong. They screened her house from the park and boat launch.

A soft trill sounded inside the house.

"Is that the doorbell?" Larry turned. "That's odd."

Larry and I stepped back inside and walked to the front door. I threw it open.

"Hello, my friends." A man with a bald head stood on the step, smiling a wide, half-crooked smile.

"Oh, hi. I'm Gary. Are you Harold?"

"That's right." He burst into laughter. "Harold the tree trimmer. That must mean that the blond-haired guy is Larry. Your other brother told me your names. Cracks me up. Terry, Gary, and Larry! Well, nice to meet you. Can I come in to take a look at our friend Tina's tree?"

Something lurched in my stomach. Tina had been very specific. No visitors allowed. But surely there was an exception for a man like Harold who had come to help. I shot a quick glance at Larry, but he was already speaking.

"Oh, yes, actually there is a gate right out front here to enter the yard." Larry pointed down to the wooden fence.

Sure enough, right beside the decorative kayak, a door opened on hinges.

"Okay." Harold shot a regretful glance past me into the house. I didn't blame him. It's fun to see other people's houses. But rules were rules.

"Are you going to remove the tree?" I walked to the edge of the porch and checked the gate into the yard. No metal lock secured it, so Harold could enter.

"Just checking it out to get her an estimate right now." Harold swung the gate open. "And I guess I'll give an old woman a good deal." He winked at me.

"That's nice of you." Larry mouthed the word *project* to me. Oh yes, Larry always remembered the project. He would have another example of someone showing love: Harold giving Tina a good deal. Larry took all the ideas.

"Oh, and watch the dog, Harold," I called. He had already disappeared around the side of the house. "He's not used to strangers."

We walked back through the house. As we stepped back on the deck, Fritz barked. Then he growled.

"Run, get food, Larry." I pointed back inside. "Let's feed him before he attacks Harold."

Larry took off for the basement. I heard his feet pounding down the stairs.

"Easy, Fritz." Terry raised the baseball bat to waist height.

Fritz ignored him. He made a lunge at Harold's pants leg.

"Ow!" Harold swung his fist at Fritz, catching him on the ear.

The Rottweiler yelped and bounded away, whining, and circled around to the deck. Larry arrived, panting, food rattling in the plastic bowl. Fritz hurried toward Larry. I stayed on the deck, watching open-mouthed as Harold rolled up his pants leg, swearing.

"You all right?" Terry rushed to his side, dropping the bat. "Did my brothers let you in? Gary!" He spun around, red-faced. "You knew better than to let a new person get close to this dog. What were you thinking?"

I hung my head.

"It's just a scratch." Harold wiped away two streams of blood with the back of his hand, which he then wiped on the grass. "Totally my fault. They warned me about the dog."

Helpless, I turned to go check on Larry.

"I need to make sure Larry's okay." I bounded into the house and down the stairs. Would the dog bite Larry too, now that he was in biting mode?

Fritz rested peacefully in his crate, panting impatiently while more dry dog food rattled into his bowl from Larry's hand.

"You okay down here?"

"Perfect." Larry set down the bowl. "Is he hurt?"

"He says it's just a scratch. But Terry yelled at me because we put him in danger. What if he sues Tina?"

"Oh, he's too nice for that. And you did warn him."

The noise of dog teeth grinding food filled the basement.

"Good night, pooch." I patted Fritz's head. "Call us if you need anything."

In the back yard, all was well. Harold finished an explanation to Terry about cutting up large trees.

"Did you come on your boat tonight?" Terry glanced toward the boat launch, invisible behind Tina's trees to the north.

"Nope. Just jumped in my truck. I'll give you a ride sometime in my boat, though."

"Great!"

"We are so sorry about the dog." Larry apologized as we all stood in the soft grass of Tina's lawn, the setting sun reflecting on our faces.

"Oh, no problem at all. It's better already." Harold waved a hand. "You know, I have an old steak in my freezer. I'll bring it tomorrow and see if I can make up."

"You think you'll be back?" Terry looked at the tree.

"Well, I haven't gotten my estimate done. I got a little distracted. You know what, guys, do me a favor. Don't tell your dad what happened. I'm just so—embarrassed, you know?"

"Oh, don't worry." I spoke, eager to make up for my wrong in letting him get close to Fritz. "It was our fault. But sure."

"Never fear." Terry waved his hand as Harold had done, as if to wave the memory away. "We won't tell."

CHAPTER SIXTEEN

More Detective Plans

W as that Harold's truck I saw down at Tina's?"

Dad looked over the salsa jar at Terry first, then at Larry and me. Somehow, all three of us had just taken a big bite of taco. And if there's anything Mom hates, it is boys chewing with their mouths open, or trying to talk while eating.

So, we took our time. I chewed and chewed and chewed, more and more slowly, hoping Terry or Larry would finish soon and answer. Apparently, they were doing the same thing.

Finally, it was getting ridiculous, so I swallowed.

"Yes, it was." I took a sip of water. "He was doing an estimate on how much it would cost to clean up Tina's tree."

"Hmm…" Dad poured a little more salsa on his plate. He reached over and did the same on Mom's plate.

Clank, the salsa jar said as he set it down.

"Why do you say hmm?" Mom asked.

I was glad she asked. I wanted to, but wasn't sure if I should. Especially since Harold had told us not to tell Dad about getting bit by Fritz.

"Oh, nothing." Dad shrugged, dipping a tortilla chip into his puddle of salsa. "It just surprises me that Tina asked him to do the estimate. She's so private. I had recommended him, but she didn't seem sure."

Mom raised her eyebrows. "Do you suspect he went on his own?"

Dad chewed slowly, as if he also needed more time to think.

"Harold's a great guy," Terry blurted out.

Two things were clear to everyone around the table.

1. We already knew Terry adored Harold and his fast boats.
2. Nobody had asked Terry's opinion.

"No, I doubt he went on his own," Dad said.

"He would have no reason to do that." My taco fell apart in my hand, and I dropped it onto my plate. "I mean, without knowing if he would get paid for his time."

"Right." Dad nodded. "Bella, this is an excellent meal."

"Thanks," Mom said, her face lighting up like the candles she loves. It's so funny because Mom and Dad got married almost twenty years ago, back in the 1960s, the same year the first man went to the moon. That seems like a long time to be married. They even argue sometimes, although usually not when we are around. Yet, they still seem to like each other, all those years later.

"I guess it's time to get dessert." Mom picked up her empty plate.

"Dessert?" Dad said. "Uh-oh. I shouldn't have eaten so many chips."

"What did you make for dessert?" Terry rubbed his stomach, as if he was starving.

"Tell you what," Mom said. "You go get it and you can be the first to know. It's down in the basement freezer in that square white container."

Mom had hit her mark. Terry usually complained about having to run an errand to the basement, but this was different. He leaped up from the table, his wooden chair skittering across the kitchen floor and crashing into the stove door. A bottle of oil on the stove tottered and somersaulted onto the chair. Thankfully, the lid was on and it didn't break.

"Oh, Terry, be careful." Mom sighed and began picking up empty plates with a snapping motion.

"Terry, you must learn to control yourself." Dad's voice broke like ice over the table.

"I was, the chair just slipped." Terry yanked the chair away from the stove and shoved it back into its place. It crashed against the table. Waves beat against the sides of my water glass.

Dad's hand dropped on to the table with more force than normal. "No, you were not. Chairs do not go flying when people get up in a controlled manner."

Terry disappeared to the basement. His feet pounded out his anger down the wooden stairs.

Mom told us boys once that Dad's anger problem used to be much worse. But because he prays a lot and listens for God's voice, he has slowly learned to fight down his impulses.

Terry got the anger problem too. And since he and Dad both have that tendency, they are usually the ones who get angry at each other.

Mom got up and put the empty plates in the sink. She passed out dessert bowls. No Terry.

"He's probably just cooling off a bit." Mom glanced at Dad. Dad nodded, biting his lip.

The silence ended with a shout from the basement.

"Fried ice cream!" The freezer door thumped shut. Terry's feet drummed up the stairs two at a time.

"Yeah!" Larry and I shouted, eager to promote peace.

Smooth, creamy ice cream. Crunchy cornflakes and chewy coconut. Brown sugar and honey drizzled on top.

The ice cream made everything better. At the end of the meal, Dad apologized to Terry for speaking so harshly. Terry agreed that he had been careless.

That night we discussed our findings from the last few days. I jotted several lines in my notebook. Larry, in his top bunk, worked on the Rubik's cube and chattered about Breguet's clocks. Terry picked up a pencil and sketch pad. Lying on his back in bed, he sketched the four ropes that connected his bed posts to the curtain rod. Once or twice in the past, Terry had catapulted out of bed and gotten tangled in one of his ropes. Another time, the curtain rod popped off its mounts and bent into a V-shape. But Terry insisted that having ropes tied to his bed were essential to his peace of mind, so the ropes stayed.

"Okay." I cleared my throat. A Rubik's cube and a sketch pad competed for the attention of my brothers. "I hereby update you on the current state of the Brady Street Boys' Map Mystery."

Somehow, saying "hereby" made my speech worthy of more attention. Terry and Larry looked up from their work.

I read my list out loud.

"One. We received a map connected to an antique clock."

"*Valuable* antique clock," Larry said.

"Likely, but please don't interrupt. Two. Raspy also told us there may be tunnels in this town. We don't know where he got his information.

"Three. Based on the information, we discovered a secret room in our own basement, containing another map similar to the first one.

"Four. We therefore conclude that the lines between the other two houses on the map may show tunnels or secret rooms."

The two maps and the old leather bag lay in the middle of our bedroom floor. We all agreed that just as soon as we solved our mystery, we would take the bag to the library. The library had a room of local artifacts, and Miss Penny would likely want to add it to the collection.

We had studied the maps until we had them memorized. We knew there were only two lines that interested us. One line went from Number Ten to Tina's basement. The other line went from Tina's basement to the river.

"So, if those lines are tunnels, where is the tunnel in Tina's basement?" Larry lay on his bunk, head dangling over the side.

We pondered this for a moment. Tina's basement had smooth cement walls covered with news clippings.

"I guess we didn't look closely." I closed my notebook. "We'll check in the morning when we let Fritz out for his run."

"Hey, that's no fair." Terry stabbed the air with his pencil. "I have to help Dad in the shop."

"You like helping him when it gets you out of other work," I said. "But since you're so whiny, I'll wait to investigate until evening when we can all go."

"Good." Larry flipped on his back and continued working on the Rubik's cube. "Because Mom will probably make me do the dishes."

Terry went back to his sketchpad.

"But how is there a tunnel from Tina's house to the river? Surely that's not what it means?" Terry put a twist into the rope he was drawing. "What good would a tunnel be if it came out under water?"

Silence filled the room, except for the scratch of Terry's pencil and the soft clicks of the Rubik's cube.

"I've got it." I slapped my notebook against my leg. "The tunnel goes into her boat garage."

Both Terry and Larry stopped what they were doing.

"Larry." Terry flourished his pencil in the air. "How did we get a brother this smart?"

"I don't know either." Larry clapped his hands. "But that's brilliant. How can we get in there to see? It's locked. Remember, we tried it before."

"Easy." Terry clapped his hands together loudly, his pencil and sketch book flying two directions. "Dive under the door. Tomorrow afternoon. I get off work after lunch."

"What about weeding the garden?" I asked.

"Oh, that's no problem." Terry gathered up his sketchpad and began searching for his pencil. "We'll weed the garden, and then Mom will let us go for a swim. Like I said, easy."

CHAPTER SEVENTEEN

A Footprint

That's how the three of us ended up in our swimming trunks beside Tina's boat garage the next afternoon, after weeding the garden.

"Is this trespassing?" Larry sat on the shore on a tangle of roots, weathered as smooth as snakes by the water.

"It doesn't say, 'No Trespassing,'" Terry said. "Anyway, we're just looking."

"I think we should dive in with a rope." I dipped my foot in the water. "It's kind of murky down there, and what if one of us got trapped?"

I had gone alone to Tina's to let Fritz out for his morning run as planned. Since we no longer locked Fritz in his kennel, he had met me on the first floor. I had not even gone into the basement.

Terry stepped onto the dock beside the boat garage and approached the side door.

"Hey!" Terry pumped his fist in triumph. "It's open."

Larry clapped his hands. He was more relieved than anyone to not have to dive into a small space.

"It was locked before, wasn't it?" I stepped onto the dock, confused.

Terry nodded, opening the door.

We peered into the garage.

"Nice boat!" Terry whistled. "What does Tina need with this thing?"

"I think her husband was the only one who used it." Larry caught up with us. "But should we tell Tina she forgot to lock the door?"

His question dissolved into the river as we moved together into the dusky interior. The shaft of light from the door pushed away the darkness as we made our way inside.

We let our eyes adjust to the darkness. There it was, as simple as can be: a door into the riverbank. Instead of a handle, it had an iron ring.

Terry tugged at the iron ring, but the door did not even budge.

"Oh, well, that's fine." He turned away. "We probably shouldn't go into someone else's tunnel, anyway."

As if it was perfectly ethical to go into someone's boat garage, but not acceptable to go into their tunnel.

That evening we hurried to Tina's house. No one spoke the words, but we were all nearly trembling with excitement about the possibility of a secret room in Tina's basement. Or secret doors that led to a tunnel to the boat garage.

We rushed past the kayak, and barely noticed the bronze owl.

Finally, Terry spoke, just as he pulled Tina's key out of his pocket. "Want to know the real problem with this? So maybe there is a secret room all cemented and stoned over like the entrance in our house. We can't go digging out the wall in Tina's house. She would flay us alive when she got back."

"Or sic her dog on us." I ran my hand up the porch pillar closest to me.

"Right."

We stepped inside Tina's house and past the porcelain dolls.

"Let's feed the dog first," Terry said, "and then while he's eating we can look around."

Fritz nearly bowled us over, but we coaxed him back down to the basement. We worked together, even though it did not take three people to feed one dog. I talked to Fritz and scratched his ears while Terry measured his food and Larry held the bowl.

"Good dog, wonderful dog, Fritz." I patted his head. "You are so handsome."

He snuffled and snorted with pleasure.

Larry took the food to Fritz's kennel.

As the Rottweiler dug in, the three of us moved to the southwest corner of the basement as if magnetized.

"If she wouldn't have put all these newspa—" Terry cut himself off short, his jaw dropping slack. He raised his hand and pointed weakly, as if his arm weighed one hundred pounds.

A padlock.

"She put the clippings up to cover the door." I breathed out the words softly as if they were dynamite.

Even after finding the padlock, it was hard to trace the outline of the door beneath the clippings. Tina's strategy—or maybe the strategy of her husband—was extraordinarily effective in camouflaging the door.

Terry, the tallest, ran his fingers lightly up the door frame to the top. "It's a door all right," he said. "Into the secret room."

"Or the tunnel," Larry said.

Our surmising ended suddenly with a sharp bark from Fritz. Upstairs, floorboards creaked as if someone had taken a heavy step.

We cocked our heads to the side, looking at each other. Fritz growled.

"What was that noise upstairs?" Terry started for the steps.

Larry shook his head, his face chalk white.

"We'd better go look." Terry started up. "We left the door unlocked, didn't we? But how would that matter just for a few minutes?"

Upstairs, we found nothing amiss.

"I wonder if we just heard some part of the house groaning." I looked into the front room to the right of the china cupboard, loaded with lace pillows and chairs from the 1950s. "Maybe—I don't know, something settled? Or the hot water heater kicked in, or..."

Terry shook his head. "The dog started barking."

"Oh, right."

"Look." Larry's chalky face had lost yet more color. His huge blue eyes fastened on Tina's carpet. Above him, the eyes of the porcelain dolls watched every move. "It's a footprint. That wasn't there when we came in."

Terry and I looked too. In the gray carpet beside the entrance, just around the corner from the china cabinet, a smudge of dirt stared up at us.

An odd, creepy feeling ran through me like a bolt of electricity. Could someone still be in the house with us now?

A noise in the basement. We all jumped. But it was just Fritz, rushing up the steps for his run outside.

"Well, I'll let him out." Terry wheeled and headed past the porcelain dolls to the back door. Larry and I followed, expecting a hand to grab us at any moment.

But nothing happened, and we all headed out into the sunshine. Laughing, we chased each other around Tina's fallen pine tree. The color returned to Larry's face. Fritz raced around the yard, barking joyfully.

About ten minutes later, we heard Harold's whistle from the gate outside the yard. We relaxed even more.

"Oh, I forgot Harold was going to bring old steak for Fritz." I punched my fist into my other hand. "And we already fed him."

Fritz barked briefly, but this time we prevented disaster. I caught Fritz's collar as Harold came around the corner.

"Hey, Harold." Terry waved. "We'd better hold off on the steak. We forgot you were bringing that, and we fed him already. Tina is really particular about Fritz not getting too much food."

"Okay, no problemo." Harold handed Terry a plastic grocery bag. "I was hoping to feed him so we'd be friends, but here you go. He can have it tomorrow."

Terry took the bag. "Hey, Harold, you didn't see anyone leaving just now, did you? We thought maybe we heard someone upstairs in Tina's house when we were in the basement."

"Didn't see anyone." Harold frowned. His bald head reflected the evening sunlight. "You probably aren't used to the noises in her house."

"There was a dirty footprint there too," Larry said.

"Really? That's strange." Harold took a notebook out of his pocket. "Or maybe you just didn't notice the dirt before. Want me to go in and help you check everything?"

Something struck me as odd when Harold said the word *problemo* and the word *before*. But I couldn't place it.

"Everything looks fine." Terry shrugged. "I think we're okay and I know you have things to do. We'll just check before we leave and make sure everything is in good shape."

"Okay." Harold walked toward the fallen tree, pen and pencil in hand. "Do you have a refrigerator to keep the meat in?"

"Yes, down in the basement, close to Fritz's cage," Terry said.

After letting Fritz run for fifteen minutes and chatting with Harold about tree cleanup, we called the dog back into the house. Larry locked the sliding doors leading to the deck, and the three of us fanned out looking for anything out of place.

"You know who I think it was?" I said. "Raspy. He's always around this neighborhood. Probably saw us come in and wanted to see what was happening."

"Could be." Terry nodded. "Then he heard the dog bark and took off."

"Well, let's be good detectives and study the dirt." I pointed to the smudge. "Maybe the next time we see Raspy, we'll be able to connect the dots."

Terry bent over the smudge. "Just dirt."

"Yeah." I squatted down on my good leg. "No Number Ten basement grime that I can tell. Let's clean it up, though. Paper towel?"

Minutes later we were walking home.

"Bottom line," Terry said, "I really want to check out the basement of the abandoned house tonight. According to the map, there is a tunnel from Tina's to Number Ten. We can't tear apart Tina's wall or break through her padlock. But maybe we can find something in Number Ten. Think we can slip over there before it gets dark?"

"Sure." I agreed, but I didn't want to. Raspy and that long knife lurked in the back of my mind.

"I just hope Raspy isn't over at Tina's." Larry looked over his shoulder at the big house.

"Nah, I'm not worried." Terry leaped up into our yard, and turned a sudden cartwheel. "Whoever came in went right back out, or Fritz would have kept barking. You know how easily dogs can smell people."

"That's true." Larry nodded with relief, flopping on our front lawn beside Terry.

I frowned at the sidewalk. I had just thought of something, when Terry said "smell people."

1. There had been no Raspy smell inside Tina's house.
2. We had arrived at the scene in less than a minute.
3. Raspy's smell lasts longer than a minute.

CHAPTER EIGHTEEN

Things Get Strange

Mom called us in for supper almost as soon as we arrived. "Corn on the cob," shouted Terry. He was passionate about food.

After we thanked God for the food, Terry selected an ear and began slathering butter on his corn.

"Gary." Mom picked up a corn cob. "The surgeon's office called today."

"Really?" I buttered my ear of corn, turning it quickly because it was still hot on my fingertips. I had almost forgotten about the letter I had written to Dr. Jefferson. "What did they say?"

Much as I hated what that surgeon had done to my leg, the idea of talking to him excited me.

"They said they got your letter and would reply later this week."

"Oh." I sprinkled salt on my corn. "Why would they call to say that?"

"It seemed a little odd to me too." Mom passed the salt-shaker to Dad, who had been patiently waiting for us to finish. "I kind of felt like she wanted to tell me something but wasn't sure if it was okay."

Mom buttered her own corn as we all munched silently.

"Well, did anyone show love today?" Mom took a bite.

We have this running dispute in our house. Do you eat a cob of corn around the ear? Or, do you eat it in straight rows, not turning the cob until you finish the entire row? Mom eats hers around, and Dad eats his in rows. The three of us try it both ways depending on our moods. Mom says her way is right because if you keep turning it, it keeps the butter from dripping off. Dad says he doesn't need extra butter.

"Gary?" Dad's voice cut through my thoughts. "How about you?"

"Me?"

"Did you show love to anyone today?"

I searched my memory. "Well, I vacuumed the floor before lunch."

"Really, Gary." Terry rolled his eyes. "First, Larry probably helped you. Second, if that's love, then Mom shows love to us every day by making us food."

"Well, she does." Dad had finished his first straight row. "Love is a decision. It's usually an action. So if you have done nothing today, you can make up for it by doing the dishes for Mom tonight."

Mom laughed. Not that she was expecting any volunteers.

"Okay, we can do the dishes." Terry set down his first cob, bare of kernels, and reached for a second.

Larry and I looked at him to see if he was serious. A couple of kernels clung to his face. But overall, his face was looking much better than it had last weekend.

"No, really, guys. We'll do the dishes and then get some fresh air before bed."

"Terry, you really have been growing up lately." Mom shook her head, as if she was slightly dazed.

But then I remembered. Possibly Terry was anxious to show Mom love. Or perhaps he wanted to keep her out of the kitchen so she wouldn't see us crawling in through the Number Ten basement window.

After we finished the corn on the cob, Dad announced he and Mom were going on a date the next evening. They planned to drive to a music program and eat at a restaurant.

"So you're tired of us?" Terry asked.

"Yes," Dad and Mom both said.

We all laughed. Who could blame them for being tired of us? And they didn't know the half.

An hour later, we were combing the north wall of Number Ten, looking for clues. The sun had not set, but it was still dusky in the basement. Larry's flashlight shone into the wooden room in the northeast corner. I was looking too, but also focusing my ears for any unusual sounds.

"Any tools around here?" Larry looked at the shelving beside the rocking chair. "Maybe we should try tapping the wall and listening for echoes."

We found a hammer in a rusty toolbox. Larry began tapping.

"You know, in our house the secret door goes out the back toward the river," I said. "This one could too."

"No. Not possible." Terry pointed to the wooden door we had found the other night. "That door opens above ground. How would you fit a tunnel in? Unless it comes up through the floor."

This drew our eyes to the floor.

And that's what we were looking at when a dog began barking.

"What's that noise?" Terry is the worst person in the world at detective work. He's the best person in the world to have along if there's a river to cross or a beast to fight or a straight wall to climb. He just can't figure out anything that involves thinking.

"It's a dog barking," I said. "It sounds pretty far away, but could it be Fritz?"

"No, it's got to be some dog outside." Terry moved back to the wall and began tapping again. "We never hear Tina's dog inside."

"True," Larry agreed.

Larry's such a nice guy, he always agrees with whatever Terry says. Terry is usually wrong.

My thoughts were these:

1. We hear Fritz barking when he runs around outside.
2. Perhaps since Tina is away, Fritz is barking inside today.

But I didn't feel like it was worth a fight. Terry could easily be right. And we had work to do, going over every inch of this wall. We also had to be ready to run if Raspy showed up.

I hoped Raspy would keep away. But I also hoped his keeping away didn't mean he was hiding in Tina's house.

We found nothing on the north wall of the abandoned basement. We didn't stay too long either, because we didn't want our parents to wonder where we were.

I think our consciences pricked us all. But we kept telling ourselves—well, I kept telling myself, at least—that we were showing love by not worrying Mom.

The next morning, I ran down to Tina's, past the wooden fence, the bronze owl, and under the eyes of the porcelain dolls.

"Come on, Fritz," I called, once inside.

No dog rushed up to meet me. Puzzled, I hurried down to his crate.

"Come on, Fritz!"

He raised his head a few inches. His black eyes pooled with sadness. Then his head dropped back onto his paws.

I squatted beside him on my good leg.

"What's up, boy?"

His chest beat out a rapid rhythm of breaths. I knew all dogs breathe quickly, but this was crazy.

I rushed up the stairs to the telephone. Tina had told us to call the vet immediately if Fritz got sick.

I wished Terry and Larry had come with me. But Terry had gone to the shop with Dad. Larry was helping Mom organize books in the library.

So I was down at Tina's calling the vet alone.

"Hmm..." the vet assistant paused. "Is it possible he ate something poisonous?"

Raspy. My mind immediately went to the footprint and last night's barking.

"I don't have any proof." My breath came fast, like Fritz's. "But it's a neighbor's dog."

"Okay. Can you get someone to bring him in?"

I said I could. Throwing the phone onto the receiver, I rushed back down the stairs.

"Come on, Fritz. We've got to go."

Coaxing him by the collar, I got him to the first floor. There, he collapsed. I shook my head and ran back to the phone. This time, I called Mom.

She said she would bring our station wagon. Larry would run down to assist me while she brought the vehicle.

We all knew it was an emergency. We could not let a dog of Tina's die on our watch.

While Larry broke a personal speed record, I rubbed Fritz's ears and begged him to stay alive.

And because of all this flurry, I did not look at the door to the secret room.

"You didn't feed him anything strange, did you?" Mom asked Larry and me as she drove us to the veterinary clinic.

We had not. Perhaps we would have if we hadn't forgotten the steak.

At the clinic, the vet team lifted Fritz on to a rolling cart. A tech with a ball point pen scratched our contact information on a registration form. They promised to take care of him to the best of their ability.

Silence filled the vehicle on our ride home. Finally, Mom spoke.

"I guess we'll still go on our date tonight. I don't think there is anything Dad and I can do for Fritz now. But I'll try to call Tina."

None of us minded that our parents would be gone for the evening. On Saturday, Mom had made extra pizza for us to warm up. Besides, we had tunnels to discuss. At least if our parents were away having fun, we wouldn't feel so bad leaving them out of everything.

Terry stayed late to close up the shop. Larry took charge of warming up the pizza and washing grapes.

I called the vet one last time before they closed.

"Midwest Veterinary."

"Hi, my name is Gary Fitzpatrick." I tried to make my voice sound official. "Could I have an update on Fritz, the Rottweiler we brought in this morning?"

"Sure, just one second," the receptionist said. She sounded like she was tired and ready to go home for the day. "Let me get you to the vet tech."

Fritz, the vet tech said, was doing okay. He had gone into convulsions a few times, but they had given him medication. They had also sedated him. He would rest well overnight.

I hated to think of Fritz's sorrowful eyes when we had arrived at the vet clinic and the staff scooped him onto a cart. Mom had tried to call Tina to let her know what was happening. But she had not answered the phone.

So there was no way to let Tina know Fritz was at the vet clinic. And we did not know why he had gotten sick.

After supper, Larry made us all help with dishes. There weren't many, just a few plates and cups and the forks we had used to shovel up pizza.

I was rinsing the last cup when Terry suggested we check on Tina's house.

"Great idea." I put the cup in the dish drainer. "We can also check Fritz's bowl and see if he ate something strange."

"And let's get the steak out of her fridge." Larry let the soapy water drain out of the sink. "We can bring it back here and put it in our freezer, and if Fritz recovers, we can feed it to him later."

"*When* Fritz recovers."

We headed down the porch steps, between the yellow marigolds, and past Number Ten. Our spirits dragged along the sidewalk, bumping against the cracks in the silence. At Tina's, the bronze owl statue eyed us moodily. He seemed to want answers from us. The stares of the porcelain dolls bored through us, as if they knew our secrets.

CHAPTER NINETEEN

Tina's Secret Room

We hurried downstairs and checked Fritz's cage. Everything looked normal. I had spilled some of his water in my morning panic. With a paper towel from the kitchen, I cleaned up the mess. Then we headed upstairs.

"Oh, I forgot the steak," Larry said. "I'll be up in a second."

Terry and I headed out to the deck to make sure everything looked in order. While Terry walked over to the fallen tree, I leaned against the deck railing and did a few things.

1. Scanned the area.
2. Worried about Fritz and hoped he would survive.
3. Thought about how the week couldn't get any worse.

Then Larry returned, and the week got worse.

You already know how Larry looks. He's thin and pale on a good day.

But tonight, right here on the deck? He was completely white.

"Larry, what's wrong?"

Larry turned the plastic shopping bag over in his hands. He looked into it.

"T-terry," he stammered. Larry never stammers. Never in my life that I can remember, besides this afternoon on Tina's porch. He's so good with words I had thought it impossible for him to mess them up.

"What?" Terry ran in behind me. He had dashed across the yard after one look at Larry's face.

"Wasn't the steak in this bag?"

Terry's eyes opened wide.

"Umm… well—did I look? I mean, I guess I did. I guess there was. I don't really remember if I looked. *Gary, did I look?*"

Terry's like that. He goes hysterical sometimes. Larry usually doesn't, but now he seemed crazy as well. I was the only person left to make decisions.

I took the bag from him. "I'm pretty sure there was steak in that bag. But—why else are you looking so terrified?"

Clearly, something more was the matter.

"The padlock is gone from the secret room." Larry spoke so low, he almost whispered. "I think someone's in there. I heard a noise."

Lots of books talk about hearts jumping into throats and ridiculous things like that. I always thought writers just made that up. Until that moment. Because my throat felt as if every one of my internal organs were cramming into it, fighting for space there.

A few important thoughts dashed into my mind like high-speed runners.

1. If the steak was missing, perhaps someone gave it to Fritz.
2. If someone gave it to Fritz, perhaps they had poisoned him.
3. Whoever gave him the steak may have poisoned him on purpose.
4. Maybe that person had been in Tina's house last night.
5. Maybe that person was in the secret room right now.

I said none of these things.

"Well, it must be Raspy," I said. "Have you seen him recently? Maybe he got into the house the other day and has been here since."

"Was the padlock on this morning?" Larry searched my eyes, hoping for a solid answer.

"I don't know. I was too busy with Fritz to notice."

Terry lifted his arm and pointed through the gap made by the fallen tree.

I frowned.

"Just watch a little—there."

Between the two evergreens, Raspy walked up the street toward Number Ten.

We stared at him stupidly. None of us wanted to find Raspy in Tina's secret room. But if it wasn't Raspy, *who was it?*

"Well, let's go see what's happening." I gave the plastic bag back to Larry and headed for the door.

The three of us walked quietly into the house and down the basement stairs.

We could see immediately what Larry had noticed. Someone had broken through the camouflaged door. The newspaper clippings hung torn and drooping on either side of the door frame.

"I don't hear anything." Terry shrugged. I could just imagine what he was thinking. *There goes Larry, hearing things again.*

Then, just like that, we heard it too.

Clank. Clank.

Terry's lips tightened. He began mouthing words to me. I had just deciphered the word *police* when a louder crash sounded in the room.

The door to the secret room swung wide.

The antique dealer. He had sunglasses on today, but I recognized his fiery red hair and mustache.

"Benjamin." I tried to keep the shock out of my voice.

"What are you doing here?" Terry asked.

Larry let out a sigh of relief. It was just his old friend, the antique dealer.

"Old lady Tina wants me to take these antiques out for cleaning. Clocks, you know. Need to be wound, stuff like that." Benjamin motioned toward the room. "As you can probably hear, I could use a little help. Want to give me a hand?"

No one spoke for a few seconds while we stared up at him, confused.

"We didn't know you found her." Terry stepped forward. "But sure, we can help."

We followed the antique dealer into the secret room.

Our eyes popped.

Jewelry dangled from peg boards. Carved antique clocks hung on the walls. Several gold mantel clocks rested on a shelf. Porcelain figurines stood together in tidy rows.

My eyes fell on a shelf below a row of clocks and ceramic figurines. Could those really be bars of gold?

Indeed, Tina's wealth was all stored here. I remembered Dad's words: "No banker knows." Tina mistrusted banks. So, this was her bank.

The room smelled of old wood and oil and something else I couldn't quite place. A kind of wood, maybe. Cedar?

"Here's what's cool," Benjamin said, swinging a door open on the far wall facing Number Ten. Behind the door was black space. It was the tunnel we had seen on our map.

"Oh wow." Larry walked toward the tunnel and peered inside. I saw rough walls and protruding rocks, similar to the secret room in our basement.

"Pretty cool, huh?" Benjamin tapped the door with glove-covered hands. "Did you like my map? Where did you put it?"

"Uh..." Larry reached into his pocket. "Nope, I don't have it with me. I guess it's at home in our room."

"Ah, well. Good. I'll show you the tunnel in a second, if you'll just help me box up these clocks. If I'm fast with my work, I can return them before Tina gets back."

"What a fun job." Larry walked to a shelf of mantel clocks. "Which ones do you want us to box?"

"These on the far wall," Benjamin pointed. "But be careful. Here's paper to pack in the boxes."

"Did you find the Breguet clock?" Larry looked from clock to clock, as if trying to remember what Breguet's looked like.

"It's got to be here somewhere." Benjamin's voice sounded irritated. "It's a little like the mantel clocks over there. Shaped like a box."

"Yes, we found a picture in a library book." Larry's eyes roamed the small room. "And those clocks can wind watches without even opening the watch."

"Yup, that Braggit was a smart man." The antique dealer picked up a mantel clock and placed it in a crate.

I wrapped a wooden cuckoo clock with paper, feeling the hair on my neck stand on end. Why did Benjamin make me feel so nervous? I felt like he was reminding me of something I could not place. Especially the way he puffed out the B in "Braggit."

"Are those really bars of gold?" Terry nodded at the lower shelf.

The antique dealer shot a glance in that direction.

"Could be," he said. "Wouldn't that be something? But of course you and I don't have any business looking at anything but the clocks."

"Right, right," Terry said.

"Pick one up and test the weight though," Benjamin said. "I'm sure she wouldn't care."

Terry reached for a bar and hefted it to his shoulder. "It's heavy, all right."

Each of us took a clock and laid it in one of the boxes. And what clocks! Pine forest and varnish and mold wafted up from them. Without doubt, they needed a cleaning. But they were exquisite. Beautiful!

"Did Tina say who made these clocks?" I let my finger slide down the curving wood.

"Nope," Benjamin said.

And just then, I saw it behind him. Another trapdoor, facing the river. It was ajar.

"Is that another tunnel?" I pointed to it.

"Yes, I suppose it is," Benjamin said, as if he had just noticed it for the first time. "Great job, boys. Want to check out the tunnel that goes toward your house? Go ahead."

Larry scampered across the room. I couldn't believe he was okay with getting in a tight space. He reached into his pocket for his ever-present flashlight and snapped it on.

I followed him into the world of uneven rock and dirt, visible only by Larry's light.

Terry lingered behind, stepping into the tunnel after both of us.

"This is great," Larry called to us over his shoulder. "I think it goes all the way to the abandoned house next door." His voice rang on the stone walls.

"Oh, I'm sure it does," Benjamin said behind us. "Check that out. Here, do you need another light?"

"Nope, Larry's got one," Terry said behind me.

His tone of voice sounded unpleasant. I wondered why he wasn't talking more kindly to Benjamin.

"Yeah, you might want to use that other exit out the other basement," Benjamin called behind us, "when you find it."

He chuckled, and we all stopped. I shivered.

"Let's get out of here." Terry turned. "Come on Gary, Larry, we're going back."

"Sorry, guys, I need this exit for a bit. You'll have to use the other one."

The door clanked shut with a bang. A dead bolt slid across it. Then another.

Then, another.

CHAPTER TWENTY

We Need an Ambulance

Above the light he was holding, Larry's eyes widened to the size they had been on the deck less than half an hour before. "What's going on?"

I wished I did not know. But suddenly, just when the man said "basement," I did.

1. I had remembered where I heard the bursting *b* sound before.
2. It was just a few days ago when Harold pronounced the words "before" and "problemo."
3. When the "antique dealer" had shut the door on us, I had seen his bright red mustache slip off his upper lip. I also noticed he no longer had the red eyebrows.

"Listen to me." I planted my hands on my hips. "That Benjamin is Harold in disguise. It's been him all along. I don't know what he's doing, but it's not good."

Smack!

A hand hit a head above and behind me in the dark.

"You're right." Terry moaned. "I knew something was wrong. When he laughed just now, he changed back to his normal Harold voice."

I went on. "Harold poisoned Fritz last night so he could break in without trouble. That's why we heard Fritz barking. I'm sure he meant to kill him."

"Are you sure that was him? How could we hear—" Terry asked.

"Maybe sound travels through this tunnel." I shook my head. "Who knows? But I am sure he poisoned Fritz with that steak."

"But why? What's going on?" Larry's light shook.

"Harold broke into Tina's house to steal her clocks and jewelry. He had to poison Fritz first so he wouldn't get attacked. Now, he locked us in here so we can't raise an alarm."

"Yes." Terry smacked his hand on his head again. "Somehow he found out a way to get to Tina's collection. He wants to get us mixed up in it so it looks like we did it. But mostly he wants us out of the way so he can escape."

Larry's flashlight shook harder, casting odd pulses of light against the rock walls.

"He's wearing gloves," I said. "So he doesn't get his fingerprints all over everything. But he made us touch everything."

Terry groaned, and I heard the smacking noise for the third time.

"But how did he get in?" Larry steadied the light with both hands. "We have the key."

"He's the one that left that dirty footprint," I said. "I'm sure of it. He probably unlocked a window so he could let himself in later."

"Look." Terry stepped past me. "Let's go as far as we can in this tunnel and talk about our options."

"Harold must be joking." Larry's voice quavered. "I thought he was a nice man. Shouldn't we pound on the door and ask him to let us out?"

"Maybe." Terry's voice came from out ahead. "But let's talk first. And, no, he just *pretends* to be a nice guy, that's all."

Terry is a little complicated, like I told you before.

1. He's not a detective.
2. He's awful at picking up on hints.
3. He grumbles about basically everything.

But, when there's a big problem to overcome, he's the man to have around.

And we had a big problem on our hands.

I motioned to Larry to follow Terry and stay ahead of me. Yes, I had the wooden leg. But from the brief glances I got of Larry's face, I feared his problem was worse than mine.

Larry hated tight spaces. He had survived the secret room in our basement because he knew he could exit when he chose.

This was different.

Also, I could feel the fine dust in the air, probably stirred up by our feet walking in years' worth of motionless dust and dirt.

Terry, out ahead, coughed.

If Terry was coughing, then Larry would soon cough. Sometimes in dust he got asthma and had trouble breathing. Sometimes in tight spaces he had trouble breathing.

But I had never seen my brother in a tight place that was also full of dust.

Ahead of me, Larry's breath quickened, like Fritz's had. He choked suddenly, and a series of coughs racked his body.

No. No!

Ahead of us, Terry turned and looked down at Larry. He bit his lips more tightly together.

"It's turning. We're almost there." He motioned to us.

Hard turn to the left. Then —

Dead end. The tunnel stopped at a wall of dirt. Terry pressed his finger into it. A small clod broke away. A tree root peered out at us.

Larry's lungs wheezed now in high musical whines. In and out. In and out.

"Don't stir up any more dirt," I said.

"I'm not stirring up dirt," Terry snapped.

"Yes, you—never mind."

"Everybody sit down." Terry dropped to the floor.

We joined him.

"You're going to be okay, Larry." I patted him on the back. "Try to focus, you know how Mom always tells you. Breathe in through your nose, out through your mouth."

"I'm going to die." Larry wheezed, desperate for air. "I—can't breathe."

Larry's eyes shone in the light like empty graves. What could we do?

"Terry, we have to go pound on the door, and tell Harold there's a medical emergency." I scrambled to my feet.

"No." Terry looked at me with piercing eyes. "Look, Larry, you will not die." Terry's voice, hard and cold, made me ache for Larry. But, I knew it might be just what Larry needed to hear. "You *are* going to pull yourself together. Gary and I will get you out of here. I'm going to search for the opening."

Terry stood, fumbling for his knife. "Gary, how about you sit by Larry and say a prayer while I work on this? We were idiots not to tell our parents."

Idiots. Yup. No question, we had been idiots.

Even when our parents came home and found us missing, would they think of checking Tina's? Would they find the secret room?

And if Terry broke into the abandoned house... what then? Would Raspy meet us with his long knife?

"Gary?" Terry's voice.

"Yeah."

"Larry should move back while I'm moving dirt."

"Just come around the corner, Larry." I got up and helped him up. "We have to get out of the dust."

Larry's breath still wheezed, but he was spacing his breaths better. I helped him relax against the passage leading back to Tina's secret room.

"I'll rub your arms and back," I told him. "That helps you relax. Move over just a little with your back toward me."

"Better pray the door isn't three feet into this mess of roots." Terry's voice mingled with the clods flying and plopping against the floor of the tunnel. "It's just nothing but dirt."

"God, we got ourselves into a terrible mess," I prayed out loud. I was really glad our parents had taught us that talking to God was as easy as talking to anyone else. But the problem was, they had also taught us that we should not treat God like a spare tire. We should have a relationship with God every day, not just when things go bad.

This felt like a spare tire prayer.

I continued, "We kept saying we were protecting our mom from worrying, and now we are trapped and our parents do not know what is going on. God, help us get out. Help Larry get better control of his breathing."

Larry lurched forward. Panicked, I tried to pull him back.

"Let me," he gasped, pointing.

"What do you want?"

"Other—wall."

Terry had been working at the end where the tunnel stopped. Suddenly I understood Larry. The opening into the Number Ten basement would be straight ahead from the main tunnel. It would not be at the end after the hard left turn.

"You're right." I scrambled up. "Terry, try this side. It must be toward the basement."

"Of course." Terry moved the light to face the south wall. "Oh, this makes way more sense."

He snagged a projecting rock, and it broke loose in his hand in a fine shower of mortar. Bad for Larry. Good for finding an exit.

"Nice thinking, Larry," I said.

"Help him." Larry motioned me to the wall.

"You sure? You okay?"

He only nodded, but I could tell that the prayer had helped defuse his rising panic. And God had spoken directions to Larry during my prayer.

I joined Terry, clawing at the rocks in the wall. A few came easily. Most of them refused to budge despite smart whacks from Terry's knife. We had no pry bar, no tools for a job like this.

"Think Raspy is in with Harold?" I asked Terry.

"Yes," Terry said, "but you don't want to listen to anything I have to say."

"You're getting us out of this, Terry." I glared at him. "So of course we want to listen to you."

He grinned for the first time since the door clanged shut on us. "Hey!" he reached his arm through a crevice. "I feel wood."

"Be quiet. If Harold thinks we are getting out, he'll—"

"He'll what?" Terry wrapped his fingers fiercely around a rock.

"Feed us poisoned steak?" I whispered, with a glance at Larry.

He was sitting at the corner, head bowed in hands, elbows on knees. Focusing on his breathing. Breathe in. Breathe out. Breathe in. Breathe out.

"He's doing okay," I said.

Terry nodded. He braced his feet on the floor and yanked at the rock with all his strength. The rock held, then gave, tumbling Terry backwards and knocking two other rocks free.

"It's nasty hard wood, though." I reached through and knocked against it. "Maybe it goes into that wooden room in the corner of the basement. But I thought that wood was removable."

"Well, we have a knife." Terry opened the blade. "It might take a while, but we'll get through by morning."

"Okay, let's do it." I breathed in deeply and began choking on the dust.

The sudden cloud of mortar threw Larry into a coughing fit too. Terry and I looked at each other again.

"We don't have all night to get him out, Terry."

Bang! Bang! Bang!

The door into the secret room reverberated with crashing fists.

"Hurray!" Terry yelled. "Someone's here to get us out."

Both of us rushed down the passage, leaving the light with Larry, guiding ourselves with fingertips on dirt walls.

"Who's there?"

"Just your friend Benjamin," the voice replied cheerfully. "I need to run an errand, but I'll be back after awhile."

"Harold, let us out of here," Terry hollered. "We know who you are."

There was a brief silence.

"Getting smart now, aren't you?" Harold snarled from the other side. "Problem is, I was smart first. Sorry, can't let you out if you're talking to me like that."

I felt my head sink on my shoulders.

"I need a little time to catch my plane to Switzerland. Got some business to do. I'm sure someone will be along to find you after a while. But first they'll search for you on the river since I sank your rowboat. They'll think you ran away or drowned. But they'll find you eventually, about the time I get my treasure locked away in Europe."

"Our brother is having trouble breathing in here." Terry's voice echoed in the tunnel. "We need to get him to a hospital."

There was no reply.

CHAPTER TWENTY-ONE

We Call for Help

I have never been so mad in my life." Terry planted both hands against the rock wall, as if he could push it away.

"Who are you mad at?" I probably shouldn't have asked that.

Terry grunted. "Okay, fine. Not just Harold. I'm mad at myself too. Does that make you feel better if you can blame me?"

"I'm not blaming you, Terry. Let's put Larry down here. That way he'll be as far from the demolition as possible."

Larry's breaths were coming fast again, much too fast.

"Come to this end." Terry took his hands off the wall and walked toward Larry. "We're going to raise a bunch of dust breaking into Number Ten."

Larry raised his head slightly. He glanced down the passage. His breath whipped in and out, in and out. His head shook, then fell on his raised knee.

Terry picked him up like he was nothing and carried him to the end of the passage and set him against the wall. He then ran back to the wooden barricade to begin destruction. If anyone could destroy a wall, it was Terry.

I paused beside my younger brother. "Larry, let me slap you on the back before I go help him."

I slapped Larry twice. A fit of coughing seized him, but that was good, I thought.

"Okay," he said when the coughing fit left. "Go."

"We're getting you out," I said. "Harold left. Don't worry about him."

I didn't bother telling him Harold had sunk our boat so people would think we had run away with Tina's treasure.

I ran back to join Terry, only to find him, rock in hand, standing in disbelief and despair.

"Beams." His lips barely parted to let the deadly word out.

I snatched the light from him and panned it over the wood.

Yup, beams. The tunnel builder had placed beams vertically and hammered planks horizontally between the beams. Two boys with a pocketknife could never move the wood structures in one night. Even if one of them was Terry.

"Dad! Mom!" I pounded on the wood with all the strength in my fists. I couldn't believe I was yelling for our parents. But perhaps they would return home early and hear me.

"What time is it?" Terry stared dully at the wall. "It's too early for them to be home, isn't it?"

"I've lost track. But this might be our only hope. We'll just have to keep yelling until they come."

"Okay. We'll take turns. You yell, and I'll work on these beams with my knife. Then, when my fingers are numb and your voice is hoarse, we'll switch."

Terry lifted his knife and dug into the wall.

"Dad! Mom! Anyone out there? Help! Help!" My voice already felt hoarse. But I knew this was not a night for normal limits. Tonight, "tired" could not be part of our thoughts.

If Terry and I had been the only ones trapped, it would have been different. We could have survived a night in a tunnel easily. But Larry—our brother. He could barely breathe. We had to get help, and soon.

In between shouts, I waited, straining my ears to hear across the wooden wall. But all I could hear was the gasping breaths from the other end of the passage, and Terry's knife nibbling at the wood.

"Not getting too far." Slivers of wood flew into the darkness. "But maybe in a few hours we can push Larry through."

"Yeah." I looked at his progress. I wanted to believe him, but the gouge he had made was not convincing.

Terry continued, trying to carve out a hole in the plank so we would have something to leverage to pull or push the plank free. I continued yelling.

"Help! Mom! Dad! It's Gary in Number Ten. We need help!"

Maybe, I thought, *someone will walk by on the street, or even up on Lexington Avenue, and hear me.*

All the while, I asked God to forgive me for hiding the truth from our parents. We had all been in the wrong together. And then, I had been stupid on my own. I had been so angry about my wooden leg that I had thought little about Larry's breathing problem. Larry had told me there is nothing more terrifying than shortness of breath. I believed him now. I believed he would take a wooden leg rather than deal with his lungs.

"HELP!"

Terry jumped.

"Warn me before you yell next time, will you?"

He was in an ill humor. Larry's life depended on Terry's knife, and that knife was not performing well against the monster plank.

I felt a vague sense of instability, like I was losing my mind. The shadowy darkness. The dust. The sound of Larry's labored breathing.

I remembered sitting at the supper table just last night, eating corn on the cob, butter and salt coating our fingers. Such luxury seemed like madness. Would there ever be a time when we would laugh and talk around a table? When we would eat good food? When we would see our parents?

Would we go mad in this tunnel? Would we ever see sunlight again? Perhaps decades from now, other boys would find this tunnel and three skeletons inside.

"Who's there?"

I am going mad, I thought, *because that sounded like a voice.*

"Who's there?" It came again, still faintly.

Terry and I stood as still as statues. The voice quavered like a—like— Raspy!

"What do we do?" In my mind, I saw Raspy's knife, glistening in the dim light of the Number Ten basement. "You think he's out to get us?"

But Terry brushed away my question. "We've got to ask him for help. Raspy! Carl! It's Terry and Gary from next door. Our brother Larry is having trouble breathing. You need to go call the ambulance."

"And tell them there's been a robbery." My voice, which had been hoarse seconds earlier, reverberated with hope.

"Ain't got no phone close by."

Raspy must be just on the other side of the wall.

"Shall we give him our key?" I whispered to Terry.

"Sure. Okay, Raspy, I'm going to make a hole in this board and push my house key through so you can go call the ambulance from our house. The hole is almost big enough."

"Okay."

"Don't leave!" I yelled at the wooden wall. "It won't take him long."

Terry gouged at the hole which was about the size of a nickel.

"Just make it longer, and it will fit."

"I know." Terry snapped at me, but he turned the knife to make an oval cut. Suddenly, the knife blade snapped and went flying. Terry yelped and held his eye.

"It got my eye, Gary. But I think it's big enough. Get the key from my pocket."

I thrust my hand into Terry's jeans pocket and pulled out the house key. I pushed it through the hole.

"Can you see it, Raspy?"

"No."

"Throw it." Terry still held his hands over his eyes. Would he go blind? It was up to me to get that key to Raspy.

It was reckless, but we were desperate. I pushed the key and heard it clang against the cement of the basement floor.

"Okay, got it," Raspy said. I heard a clink as he picked it up. "I'll go to your house and call the ambulance."

We rushed to the other end of the tunnel. We assured Larry that help was coming. But in my mental notebook I made a list of the things that might go wrong.

1. Raspy might vandalize our house and never call.
2. Raspy might be in league with Harold and give the key to him.
3. Even if Raspy called, would the 911 operators believe him?
4. Even if the medics got here, could they get Larry out in time?

Wheeze. Wheeze. Wheeze.

Larry's breathing sickened me. Where was Raspy by now? Surely many minutes had passed since our key clattered onto the basement floor.

"Terry, what time of day do you think it is now?" We both slumped beside Larry on the tunnel floor.

"No idea."

We had debated trying to keep hacking our way out through the wooden wall. But with the pocketknife broken and Terry's eye dripping blood, we counted instead on Raspy's good graces and God's mercy. I could not chew through the boards with my teeth.

"Doing okay, Larry? Help will be here soon, I'm sure." I rubbed his arm again.

"Okay."

I turned to Terry. "Do you think Tina ever even called him about the tree?" I didn't bother saying who I meant by *him*.

Terry stared at me through the darkness. I could imagine drops of blood sliding down the fading purple under his eye.

"You might be right. He lied about her asking him to clean the clocks, so why not about the tree too?"

"Hmm. I hadn't even thought about what Tina will say. We are finished."

"Yup." Terry rubbed his back against the wall. "But as long as we all get out of here alive, I'll go to jail gladly."

"Her treasure room." I held out my fingers, creating a list. "Her dog. Her house. We ruined everything. And she didn't like us to begin with."

We fell silent, contemplating our fate.

Terry finally spoke. "How did Harold know that Tina has clocks and tunnels? We didn't even know."

I had no answer, but I had another question. "Is Harold

really an antique dealer and a tree trimmer?"

Terry frowned. "I don't know."

"No," came a weak voice from my other side.

"Larry, you shouldn't even be talking." I turned his direction.

"He—said—it wrong."

Terry and I stared at Larry.

"Oh, Breguet." I could almost hear Harold saying *Braggit*. "That's right. He said it wrong and spelled it wrong. A real antique dealer would know the correct way."

We sat.

We waited.

"Hey, what's that?" Terry stiffened beside me. "I thought I heard—"

"A siren." I leaped to my feet. "Larry, the ambulance is here. You'll be fine!"

Larry just nodded.

"I'll run to the wooden wall in case we have to direct them." Terry was on his feet too. "But they'll have to come down through Tina's house."

I waited beside Larry as Terry ran to the other end of the tunnel, taking the light. Soon I heard him yelling.

"Are they going through Tina's house? Okay, good."

Surely Harold was gone by now. I hoped the EMTs would not get into any trouble coming through the house.

"Hello?" A faint voice called. "Hello?"

"This way," I shouted.

"Pound on the door." Terry yelled, rushing down the passageway. "Raspy says they're coming."

We beat on that door like it was our own stupidity. I think blood would have shortly spurted from our fists. But the door suddenly swung open and a powerful flashlight blinded us.

CHAPTER TWENTY-TWO

Help Arrives

Is there an ambulance here?" Terry blinked into the light. "Larry needs to go to the hospital."

The uniformed man nodded, barking into his radio. It was Officer Jackson. Two EMTs burst into the secret room with a stretcher. Terry and I dragged Larry from the tunnel.

"You're saved, Larry." I heard a crack in my voice, but I wasn't embarrassed, just glad.

A firefighter in full gear puffed in after the EMTs. Together, the three professionals hooked Larry up to a breathing mask connected to a green oxygen tank. Gloved fingers, again. This time, turning the dial on the oxygen tank, giving Larry life.

"There's been a break-in." Terry turned to Officer Jackson. "A man named Harold just stole a bunch of stuff from the woman who owns this house. He locked us in the tunnel. He's probably escaping by boat. He went out that way." Terry pointed to the door in the wall leading to the river.

"We heard there was a break-in," Officer Jackson said. "I called for the police boat, and it is heading this way from Main Street."

"It's probably passing Harold," Terry shouted. "He'll be heading that way, I'm sure."

The EMTs slowly made their way up the basement steps with Larry. We ran upstairs to Tina's back deck, which gave a partial view of the river between the trees.

After the closeness and darkness of the tunnel, I didn't know what to do or where to go or what to think about first.

1. I rejoiced that we were out of the tunnel.
2. I mourned the theft and the poisoned dog.
3. I worried about what our parents and Tina would say.
4. I still worried about Larry, even though he was in excellent hands.

Nothing was visible on the river. I ran back into Tina's house to watch the stretcher heading down the porch steps.

"Is he going to be okay?" I asked the closest EMT.

"Oh, he'll be just fine in no time. Just needs to catch his breath."

I watched the crew load Larry in the ambulance and drive away. I headed back into the house. I paused for a moment, under the eyes of the porcelain dolls.

"Thank you, God. Thank you."

I headed down the hall. The door behind me burst open and our parents rushed in. The date was over.

"What is happening?" Mom's face looked like wax. "Why was there an ambulance out front?"

"Gary! What's going on? Where are your brothers?" Dad said.

After a few minutes of this, we untangled the people and questions. Mom went to the hospital to join Larry. Dad and I hurried onto the back porch to see what Terry was doing.

Officer Jackson watched the river, his radio crackling.

"We are gaining on the suspect right at this moment, but we're going to need backup. Jackson, did you alert Boat Two?"

"Ten-four, I did," Officer Jackson said. "Does he appear to be armed?"

"Not sure."

Just then we heard the whine of a boat motor. "I hear two motors," Dad said. "I think it's the chase."

We held our breath. Fifteen seconds later, Harold's boat shot around the bend. It flew across the water, spray showering around and behind it. A hundred yards behind, the police boat pursued, sirens wailing.

"His boat is heavy, but he's gaining on them," Dad said. "He races boats. He knows what he's doing."

But then, from the Lexington Street Bridge, we heard another boat motor. A second police boat appeared under the bridge.

"They've trapped him." Terry clasped his hands together.

But Harold was not so easily defeated. His motorboat swung left, then right, then left, zigzagging so rapidly that I couldn't believe the looted treasure could stay inside. Then Harold's boat headed straight for the oncoming police boat.

"They're going to crash!" I gripped the deck railing.

The police boat swerved left. Harold swerved too, and shot past the police boat.

"He got away." Terry's voice dropped like a popped balloon.

"Not possible," Officer Jackson said. "He won't be able to dock and run. They've got him."

"And the first police boat gained ground while he was swerving," Dad said.

The whine of the boats moved out of earshot. Officer Jackson continued talking back and forth with other officers.

Dad turned to Terry and me. I was expecting him to scold us within an inch of our lives. We deserved it. But he just put one arm around Terry and one arm around me and bowed his head. He prayed the same prayer that I had prayed.

"Thank you, God."

Tears rolled down my cheeks like they would never end. It was no use trying to fight them off. I guess it was okay, though, because Dad shed a few tears too. Even Terry's eyes glistened, as he ran his hands through his hair.

Officer Jackson called for backup and began going through the evidence at the house. We followed him down to the secret room. Harold had left one bar of gold, along with several broken clocks.

Another officer joined him. They needled us with questions.

"He told us to pick up the clocks and look at them." Terry shook his head. "I didn't think about it that he wanted our fingerprints on them. So these will probably have our prints all over them. He was wearing gloves."

"Do you have any idea if the owner of the house knew this man?"

We both looked at Dad.

"I don't have any reason to think so." Dad frowned. "I suggested him to Tina for cutting up her tree, but I don't believe they met."

Officer Jackson nodded. The other detective scrawled something on a yellow legal pad.

"We have apprehended the suspect," a voice crackled over the radio. "Suspect and one police officer injured in gun fight, no fatalities. Injured suspect will be en route to hospital under police guard."

"Gun fight?" I felt my old panic rising. "They won't put him next to Larry in the hospital, will they?"

"He won't be able to do any harm," Officer Jackson said. "He's already in handcuffs."

"Okay." Dad exhaled as if he had been holding his breath for the last half hour. "It's time someone called Tina."

Sometimes nothing is as nice as sitting in a room with your family, even past midnight.

Larry had revived in the emergency department. He now lay curled up on the couch, his yellow hair falling over his forehead. And his breathing?

Normal. I couldn't even hear it from my position on the carpet.

"I feel like Daniel fresh out of the lion's den." Larry swung his arms in a wide arc of joy.

"What are you saying, that we're lions?" Terry growled. But his growl sounded like a smile.

The world had righted on its axis.

Well, most of it. There were still some problems left.

1. We didn't know what Tina would say.
2. We expected punishment from Dad and Mom.
3. Fritz was still lying in the animal hospital, trying to recover.
4. There was no sight of Raspy, our hero.
5. There was no sight of the *London*, our boat.

"So." Dad raised his feet in the recliner. "How do we ask questions? I'm sensing that you boys have been hiding some things from us."

One of those silences followed where we each hoped the others felt like talking. No one opened his mouth, so I went back to thinking about what I could say myself if I started talking. But there was still no talking.

Finally, Terry spoke. He was lying on the carpet as usual, his feet resting on the arm of Larry's couch. The knife blade flying at him had left a swollen eye, but we discovered that it nicked his eyelid, and not the eyeball. It fit in nicely with his other injuries from last Friday.

"It was my fault." Terry rolled over and sat up. "We found the tunnels under the houses. We didn't want to scare Mom, but we should have just told you."

"Houses?" Mom said. "What other house? What other tunnel besides the one going from Tina's to the abandoned house?"

We studied the ceiling.

"Our house," I said.

"Ours?" Dad and Mom said together.

"Well, just a secret room," Terry said. "It's not a tunnel, so it's not a big deal."

But, apparently, it was a big deal to them.

We all went down to the basement. We showed our parents how the wooden shelves came forward, revealing the hole that led to the secret room. Then we all went back to the living room. Terry ran upstairs to get the leather bag and the map, and showed them to Dad and Mom.

"We also sneaked out of the house once to check out the Number Ten basement," I offered, getting bolder the more adventures we confessed. "Raspy was down there, but I don't think he saw us."

Mom turned paler with each new story.

"Does he sleep down there?" Dad bit his lip, thinking. "I question whether you should be afraid of him. He saved you tonight."

"Right." Terry was collapsed flat on the carpet again. "We thought all the time that he was the bad guy. We even thought he might have robbed Tina. Nope. Harold the entire time."

"Well," Dad said. "We'll have to finish this discussion tomorrow. I have a few things to share after talking to Tina on the phone. But I think I will talk to your mother first."

"Things to share?" Terry shot upright again.

"Yes," Dad said. "But that will wait. And we will have to discuss what consequences fit boys who sneak out of the house without permission."

"And hide things like secret rooms and maps and red-haired visitors," Mom added.

"Oh no," Terry groaned.

None of us were surprised, though.

"I think I did the wrong thing by calling Harold about Tina's trees." Dad yawned. "There was something that made me uneasy about him. Like that time he told you about racing his boats, Terry. The whole time he was talking to you, he was drinking a beer."

So that's what Dad had meant by people who teach teenagers bad habits.

"I'm just glad everyone is okay." Mom wiped her eyes.

And Dad thanked God again before we went to bed.

CHAPTER TWENTY-THREE

Raspy Tells His Story

S everal things needed attention on Thursday.

1. We called the vet. Fritz was recovering. Life was good.
2. Mom and Dad settled on our punishment: sanding and painting the porch. Our porch is huge, with lots of spindles. Life was grim.
3. Raspy walked over to our house to check on Larry.

The three of us ran to the porch.

"Thanks for helping us last night!" We circled around Raspy, stench and all.

"Yes, you saved us," Terry said.

Larry grinned widely.

"Next time you want to come visit me in that basement," he rasped out from beneath his cap, "just come over and say hi the reg'lar way."

We all laughed.

"Instead of coming through the tunnel, you mean." I nodded with understanding.

"Or the basement winda."

Oops.

"Were you awake when we escaped through the window?" I looked wide-eyed at Terry and Larry.

"Yup!" His eyes brightened with pleasure. "And when you crawled into the basement through the winda. Right across the street. I waited and waited for you to come back out so's I wouldn't scare the living daylights outta y'all. But you wouldn't come, so I finally comes down to the basement anyways, and I sees ya standing like them scared rabbits under the winda. So I snores real loud so you would know you could go."

Our mouths fell open like broken toys. None of us could speak.

"Don't never need to worry about me," Raspy said. "I just pulled that knife out for a joke."

That did it. We burst out laughing. We had stood frozen in that wretched basement, while Raspy had been trying to scare us.

"Anyways, d'y'all think your mom gots a sandwich for me?"

I turned to find Mom. Where was she? Right behind us, listening and smiling.

"I'll get you a sandwich, Carl," she said. "But, Carl, why were you in that house? Do you own it?"

"Harold owns it, ma'am."

Our jaws dropped again.

"He told me I could stay in there if I help him look for the tunnel."

Mom looked at Raspy without speaking for a minute.

"So Harold sent you in there to look for tunnels?"

"Yes, ma'am." Raspy frowned and fidgeted, his feet shuffling on our weathered porch floor. "We didn't know he was looking for tunnels to break into the old lady's house. He just said he was part of that there historical group. I wouldn't tell you now, 'cept I guess if he's in jail, he won't come get me."

"Well, I declare," Mom said. "I wonder what will happen to the house now that the police arrested Harold."

The three of us shot nervous looks at each other. Mom would not be interested in staying here if Harold owned the house next door.

Then again, we might not want to live here either.

We chatted with Raspy while Mom made him a sandwich. Then he waved, wished us a good day, and walked toward the park at the end of Brady Street, munching bread and ham.

"Now I understand why Harold and Raspy both talked to us about the tunnel," I said. "Harold hired Raspy and a bunch of other guys to look for his tunnel."

"Do you think Harold was in the group that went into the house?" Larry sank in a wicker chair, and leaned against the peeling porch railing. He was fully recovered, but still tired from yesterday's strain.

"I doubt it." I sat in the chair beside him. "He didn't want to make himself look guilty."

Dad had run to the shop, promising to be home by noon.

After Raspy left, we set out to find the *London*. We found that the sunken rowboat had caught on a fallen tree, which kept it from floating away. Terry ran up to our bedroom and unfastened the four ropes from his bedposts.

With them tied together, we pulled the *London* up to the sunlight once more, turning it upside down to dry.

When Dad's motorboat came within sight, Mom started grilled cheese sandwiches. By the time we had all washed up, the aroma of toasted bread and cheese filled the house. We sat down to eat and listen to Dad's story from Tina.

"So, Tina tells me she knows Harold." Dad took a sandwich and passed the platter to me.

"What?" I almost dropped the plate.

"Turns out, he is the thief her husband fired from the clock company years ago."

"Whoa!" Terry yelled.

"Not so loud," Mom said.

"When I told her what happened, she said Harold was a good friend of her husband's before he found out that the man was a thief. Harold knew about Herbert's collection of valuable clocks and the secret room and the tunnels."

Dad paused and took a bite.

"One time after Harold left their house, a map of the tunnels was missing. When Herbert asked Harold if he had seen the map, he said he had not. But soon after, money disappeared at the clock company and Harold went to prison. That's when Herbert put deadbolts all over the house and in the boat garage."

"Right, how did Harold get into the secret room?" Larry set down his sandwich as if it was too much for him. "They padlocked it."

"He's an experienced thief," Dad said. "He cut the lock."

"And he got into the house by sneaking in one day when we were there," I said. "We think he unlocked a window so he could get in later. We were blaming Raspy the whole time."

"But why didn't he come in through the tunnel from the river?" Larry picked up his sandwich to make another attempt.

"Deadbolts," I said. "I bet it had three deadbolts just like the one in the other tunnel. He could open those once he was inside the secret room and use it for an escape route. And he could load his boat in the garage out of sight."

"You can also tell he knows a lot about stealing because he wore gloves," Terry said.

"And he's such a smooth liar, he must have lots of practice." I wrapped the stringing cheese around my bread. "But he didn't have much practice coloring his hair. I can't believe we didn't realize it was fake the first time."

"And I don't see how he thought the police would blame you." Mom shook her head. "Even if you touched the gold and had the tunnel map."

"Did he buy Number Ten just to make it more likely that he could rob Tina?" Larry fiddled with a golden triangle of broken bread before popping it into his mouth.

Dad nodded. "Tina said it's very possible that he only came for that. Maybe he thought there would be an opening from the Number Ten house. Since she left town, he got a chance to break in through her house. She apologized over and over for putting you boys in harm's way."

All three of our heads—Terry's curly one, my brown one, and Larry's yellow one—shot up.

"Apologized?" Terry's last bite of sandwich suspended in mid-air. "I guess you forgot to tell her about Fritz."

"No, I told her," Dad said. "And that was last night when we didn't know how Fritz was doing. But she understands that three boys are more important than one dog. She'll be home this afternoon."

"This sounds like a good time to think about our fruit of the Spirit project." Mom got to her feet and picked the poster board off the refrigerator, snapping the magnet back in place. "Who showed you love in the last few days? And how did you show love back?"

We fell silent again. Mom makes people think *way* too hard.

Larry spoke first. "Gary and Terry showed love to me." His thin face beamed. "I'm not sure I would have survived without them."

A tear slid down Mom's face, then another, but her pen flashed down the column on the poster board.

Did we really help save Larry's life? I wondered.

"I know someone who didn't show love," Terry said. "We won't name him. Mom, can we have the leftover fried ice cream?"

"That would make a great half-time snack while painting the porch."

"Ohhhh."

Isn't it just the worst when you keep forgetting a chore you need to do, and so you have to keep remembering it all over again?

"Who was the most surprising person who showed you love?" Mom kept jotting on the chart.

"Raspy!" I said. "We totally guessed him wrong."

"And Tina, if she's really not mad at us." Larry spoke the words slowly, as if speaking them would make them false.

Mom pulled out Oreo cookies so we could satisfy our sweet tooth before our big job.

"Remember how Larry said that the North Star is a good symbol of love?" I asked. "Our flashlights were like that too, in the tunnel."

Mom nodded, pleased.

"Light shows things as they are," she said. "No secrets. Which symbol shall we use for love?"

"I like the flashlight idea." Terry popped an Oreo cookie in his mouth, whole. "We would have been in big trouble without Larry's flashlight."

"Terry, don't talk with food in your mouth." Mom frowned. "But your idea is good. Do you want to draw the flashlight?"

Terry waved a hand at me. "Let Gary do it. I only draw ropes. He draws everything."

"Okay," I said. "I'll draw the flashlight."

"Okay, Gary." Mom looked at me. "Try to get the drawing done tonight. We need to wrap this one up so we can move on to joy, the second fruit."

We heard a knock on the door.

"Raspy again?" Terry suggested, his mouth still full of cookie.

CHAPTER TWENTY-FOUR

Tina Tells Her Story

D ad left the table and opened the door. The rest of us followed.

"Tina!" He motioned her inside. "Come in and sit down."

The little German lady walked right in. She perched on the edge of our couch.

"I am so glad you boys are okay," she said. "If I would know zat man was close by, I would never have let you be in his way. He is bad, wicked man."

"Did he steal all your things?" I sat on the floor, absorbing every word. "He sank our rowboat. But we pulled it up."

"Police get my zings back." Tina's face broke into a smile. "But, anyway, I had already taken zee clock he was looking for to my son's house."

Our eyes widened.

"Back when my husband and zis man work together, some man donate a clock that some people say be made by French man named Breguet."

"That's what Harold wanted. He pretended to be an antique dealer and tried to get us involved." Larry quivered with excitement. "I read about Breguet's clocks in a book."

"He probably want me to blame you," Tina said. "Yes, Harold want zis clock. We put zee clock in our secret room until we have time to call expert. Zen my husband die, and I leave clock in room. Just last week, I remember clock. I zink, if zis thief get out of prison soon, he come find clock. So I go down to room and get clock. I take to my son to get in safe place. We take to expert. To see if Breguet make zis clock."

"But how did you get into the room without moving the newspapers off the door?" Terry looked up from the floor.

"I take off," Tina said, eyeing Terry askance. "I open door. Zen, I put papers back on."

"Smart!" I said, hoping to make up for Terry's nosiness. Tina was being very nice to us, and there was no point in ruining it.

"We take to expert," Tina said. "But it is imitation. Not Breguet."

"Oh, that's too bad," Larry said. "How can they tell?"

"Zee little gears and wheels," Tina said. "Not like his. So Harold risk his life for clock zat is not even real."

"And something that you had already taken away," I said.

Tina twisted a strand of her cottony white hair, as if she were searching for a thought in her brain.

"I give you boys gift for all your trouble."

I gulped. I heard both Terry and Larry inhale sharply.

"Oh, I don't know—" Dad began.

"No, no, please," she said. "I do zis. My husband has motorboat in storage since he died. Leetle rusty. You are mechanic, you fix. But I vant zese boys to have it."

Behind me, Terry sucked in most of the air in the living room.

"Tina." Dad cleared his throat. "I really appreciate this, but your husband's motorboat was worth quite a bit. Beautiful boat—"

"Exactly." Tina smiled patiently. "And I get old. I move to my son's house soon. I give boat to zese boys."

We all shot a glance at Dad.

"Well, say 'thank you,'" he said, as if we were three years old and had forgotten our manners. When really, we were still waiting to see if he would let us accept the gift.

"Hurrah!" Terry yelled. That's the way he says thank you.

"Can we name it?" I wrapped my arms around my knees, to keep myself grounded.

"Sure," she said. "My husband put number on it, but no name."

Big Ben." I clapped my hands, unable to restrain myself. Finally, a boat big enough for the name.

"Thanks for asking our opinion." Terry rolled his eyes. But it was all for show, because he didn't care about names.

"Sure, that is a great name," Larry said. "When can we go see *Big Ben* again?"

"Again?" Dad looked at Larry.

Larry's eyes fell.

We all shifted. We had forgotten to confess that detail.

I decided to do the honors and speak first. Terry had done it last night. "We just peeked our heads in. It wasn't locked."

"Just wanted to see if there was a door into the riverbank." Terry motioned with his arms as if that made our decision reasonable.

"Don't vorry, don't vorry." Tina laughed. "Boys like to see zings. Zey knew it vould be zeirs soon."

"Well, Tina, we are punishing them for not talking to us about all of this," Dad said.

"Yes, we have to sand and paint this whole porch," Terry waved a hand toward the front door. "Every single spindle, and there are about a million."

"Good, good." Tina got to her feet. "Good job for boys. Now, I need to check Fritz. He come home today. Come down zis afternoon and I give you key to boat garage and boat."

"But, Tina," Terry could not restrain himself. "Did you know there were tunnels under your house?"

How could she not know, if she knew about the secret room? I thought. But Terry didn't think.

"I know." Tina looked back at Terry. "When we buy property, owner tell us about tunnels and cellars. He give us map. He say for Underground Railroad, but Herbert not zink the tunnels that old. Maybe just for storage. Sometime I show tunnels to museum, they figure out."

"Tina." One other thing bothered me. "When we were biking in the street last week, did you call the police to tell us to get out of the street?"

"No." The little lady's eyes opened wide. "But boys should not play in zee street."

"I thought so." I leaped up, thrilled with my discovery. "Harold called the police on us. I bet he wanted the police to think we were bad guys. Then, if there was a robbery, the police would blame us, the naughty boys."

"Ahhhh!" Terry said. "Here we were mad at Tina the whole time and it was Harold."

"Well, Terry." I glanced at Tina. "We weren't exactly *mad* at her."

I could just see what might happen if this conversation continued. Tina would change her mind about giving us *Big Ben*.

"You can be mad." Tina smiled again. "I just a grouchy old voman. Okay, I go. Goodbye!"

All five of us stared after her.

Dad turned toward the kitchen. "I have never heard her talk so long with no complaints about the United States."

Back at the table, Terry grabbed another cookie. Larry and I followed.

"I feel like King Solomon in the Bible." Larry took a gulp of water. "We're rich! Mom, add Tina to the chart."

"I can tell you who is not rich." Dad reached for an Oreo cookie. "Well, besides you. Tina also told me that Harold is deep in debt. We are sure he was hoping to sell her Breguet clock on the black market. Since that fell through, they will put all his possessions on the sheriff's auction. I'm guessing Number Ten will get taken down."

"Oh." I looked at Dad. "So if there isn't a creepy house next door, we get to stay here, right?"

Dad raised his eyebrows. "First, we have to make sure that our boys are learning the fruit of the Spirit rather than creeping around the neighborhood."

My eyes fell. Thankfully, the telephone rang just then.

Mom stood up to get it. "Oh, yes. Yes. Would you like to talk to him? Oh."

There was a silence.

"Oh. Okay, I'll let him know. Yes, that would be nice. We might just do that."

She hung the phone on its cradle.

"That was the University of Chicago." Mom seated herself at the table. "Dr. Jefferson's office."

"Oh," I said. "Do I get to go see him now?"

I didn't feel nearly as angry toward him as I had a few days before. Before the horrible evening in the tunnel. But now that Mom had suggested I talk to him, I was pretty excited about it.

"Well..."

She stopped.

Now this was strange. Mom is the quietest person in the house. But when she says something, she means it. And she rarely starts a sentence if she can't finish it.

So we all looked at her.

She frowned, and her forehead wrinkled. "He's not there anymore. But the receptionist invited us to come up and look at your records."

"Oh, yes, let's go to Chicago," I said.

"Is he working at a different hospital?" Dad asked.

"I was going to ask that, but she said no one knows where he is right now. Just that he isn't working there anymore. It's strange. But again, I felt like she was—not saying quite everything."

"Is Dr. Jefferson a criminal?" The muscles in my neck contracted.

"Oh, I doubt it," Mom said.

"I still want to talk to him."

"Let's all plan a day trip to Chicago," Dad said. "We can take the train and visit the university hospital. I'm sure they will help us find him."

"Another adventure." Terry clapped his hands together. "Let's plan it out this afternoon."

"No," Mom said. "Let's get started on the porch this afternoon. That's what you're doing next."

Dad looked us all over slowly, his eyes moving from Terry, to me, to Larry. "Don't forget what you learned. First, not everyone who appears loving really is. Sometimes it takes time to find out the truth. Second, a big part of love is honesty and openness. If we want to have good, loving relationships with people, everyone needs to be open and honest. No secret tunnels or night escapades."

We chewed on our cookies, saying nothing.

"Love, no secrets." Terry drummed a rhythm for the phrase on the table. "Can we paint that phrase onto the front of the house?"

I looked at Dad. He looked as if he were about to laugh. "No."

"Oh, come on." Terry let his head fall against the table as if crushed.

"Time to get going." Dad pushed his chair away from the table. "I'll make plans for our trip to Chicago and go look at the boat when Tina comes back. Bella, maybe if our porch gets a new paint job, we won't have to move."

He winked at Mom, and we all shouted with triumph.

"Hurray! We don't have to move!"

"Go get your brushes." Mom picked up the poster board and clipped it back into its spot on the refrigerator.

"Well." I got up and headed for the basement stairs. "I hate to admit it, but I've never been so happy to have a big job to do. It's better than going to jail."

"You can say that again." Terry jumped in the air, reaching to touch the ceiling. He can't reach it yet, but he always tries. "I think I'll run out and do a cartwheel in Brady Street."

"I feel as happy as the children of Israel when God parted the Red Sea." Larry, breathing normally, followed me to the paint room.

If you need us, we'll be painting the porch!

Find the rest of the books in this series as they come out by visiting *www.katrinahooverlee.com* and subscribing to our email list.

About the Author

Hi! I'm Katrina.

When I was a little younger than Terry, Gary, and Larry, I created them to help pass the time doing chores. I told stories about the boys to my brother Scott as we weeded the driveway, worked in the produce patch, or folded laundry. Occasionally, Mom even banned the storytelling because it took us longer to do our work if I was telling stories!

For about a decade, I wrote books for adults, including *Blue Christmas, Shatterproof, Captain Garrison,* and *From the White House to the Amish.* You can browse my books at my online store, as well as in many other stores.

Now my husband Marnell and I have a child of our own. Upon the suggestion of my aunt Virginia, I am returning to my own childhood and bringing Terry, Gary, and Larry back to life. My husband lost his leg to cancer as a young boy, so I return to his childhood as well, even though the stories are different from Marnell's life.

My husband and I currently live in Elkhart, Indiana, close to the fictional town of Stratford. I named the boys' town after my hometown in Wisconsin. It is set on the St. Joseph River, right between South Bend and Elkhart. Although it is real in this story, do not come to northern Indiana looking for the town of Stratford. You will not find it!

To keep up to date on more books in this series, subscribe to my email list at *www.katrinahooverlee.com*. You may also write to Katrina Lee, The Brady Street Boys, PO Box 2155, Elkhart, IN 46515.

Did you enjoy *Trapped in the Tunnel*?
Are you able to leave an online review?

Today, many people buy books online. Your review is crucial to help others know what a book is like. These reviews also help people like Marnell and me who are producing our own books. No matter where you bought your book, if you could take a few moments to give an honest review on Amazon or another online store, it would help us a lot.

Thanks!
Marnell and Katrina

Many Thanks!

- My husband Marnell, who inspired and directed the writing of this book many times.
- Editors: Sherilyn Troyer, Gideon Yutzy, Esther Yutzy, and Gina Martin. There would be no Book One without you!
- Illustrator Josh Tuft, for your fantastic work.
- Designers Tobi Carter and Viewfinder Creative.
- Alpha readers: Alyssa Hoover, Bensen Slabaugh, and Dracko Carlin, the very first readers of *Trapped in the Tunnel*.
- The many beta readers from around the country and the world. See the list following. These young people (ages 8-16 on average) read the book and completed a questionnaire to help me make decisions about the book.

Beta Readers

Adam Loewen .... Manitoba, Canada
Jeneva Yoder ....,....................... Ohio
Jana Gerber.. Ontario, Canada
Cole Miller ....Missouri
Laurel Petre.. Pennsylvania
Jenna, Heather, and Molly Derstine .... Mississippi
Vince & Quinn Graber .... California
Anthony Yoder.. Ohio
Darren Yoder .... Ohio
Sylvia Dyck.. Ontario, Canada
Georgiana Graber.. Mississippi
Deborah Brubaker.. Wisconsin
Kaylie Kauffman .... Kentucky
Vinton Martin.. Maryland
Wade Brubaker.. Wisconsin
Brooke Mummau .... New York
Olenka Hursh.. Krivoshiyentsy, Ukraine
Dawson Yoder.. Rustburg, VA
JahZemira Beachy .... Belize
Tyrell Rosenberry .... Pennsylvania
Zafira Beachy .... Belize
Jessalyn Eby.. Colombia, South America
Samantha Duerksen .... Manitoba, Canada
Tristan Zook.. Pennsylvania
Monica Yoder .... Ohio
Jamison Steinmann .... Kentucky
Lane Yoder.. Mississippi
Zeke High .... Pennsylvania

Rebecca Miller...Nebraska

Ashlyn Zimmerman ....Oklahoma

Jaxon Petre ....Ohio

Tessa Reinford ....North Carolina

Kurtis Loewen ....Manitoba, Canada

Jeriah Goff..Belize, Central America

Cheyenne Graber...Missouri

Victoria Miller ....Mississippi

Lydia Miller...Nebraska

Jamin Miller...Missouri

Anna Miller...Nebraska

Maria Brubacher...Pennyslvania

Kaitlyn Siegrist ....Pennsylvania

Genevie Leinbach ....Indiana

Julie Leinbach...Indiana

Meghan Leinbach..Indiana

Erika Leinbach ....Indiana

Cassidy Leinbach...Indiana

Adrielle Frost ....Belize, Central America

Nicki Lapp...Mississippi

Jayron Penner ....Manitoba, Canada

Kaylene Penner..Manitoba, Canada

Sarah Martin, Philip Martin, Clarisa Martin, Rebekah Martin................ Indiana

Patrick Steinmann .... Kentucky

Elliot Mast..Pennsylvania

Rachelle King... Morgantown, Pennsylvania

Katie Schrock .... Mississippi

Virgil Kauffman ....Pennsylvania

Conrad Lapp .... Mississippi

Daryn Kauffman .... Mississippi

Corbyn Strite..Pennsylvania

Charlotte Sommers .... California

Caleb Lapp .... Mississippi

Katelyn Zimmerman ....Pennsylvania

Jason Miller .... Romania

Lee Alan .... Mississippi

Curtis Friesen .... Belize

Hannah C. Yoder .... Indiana

Vance Kolb .... Pennsylvania

Blake Brubaker .... Pennsylvania

Ivan Strite .... Virginia

Tivon Kolb .... Pennsylvania

Ayden Shirk .... Missouri

Carlin Shirk .... Missouri

Jacob Hege .... Georgia

Sophia Petre .... Ohio

Aleah Zimmerman .... Pennsylvania

Kiersten Miller.. Mississippi

Lincoln Fleagle .... Mississippi

Missie Miller...Oklahoma

Hadassah Yoder .... Oklahoma

Taylor Knepp .... Oklahoma

Bryant Yoder.. Oklahoma

Jalisa Zimmerman .... Oklahoma

Marlissa Halteman .... Pennsylvania

Stewart Noble Kurtz.. Nakuru, Kenya

The fifth and sixth graders from the Krivoshientsi School: Amanda Stoltzfus, Miroslava Fed, Veronica Kolesnik, Sonya Snopkov, Dosha Tyschenko, Bogdonna Kosenko, Marina Stoltzfus, Margaret Miller .... Ukraine

Arwen Zook .... Pennsylvania

Ginevra Zook .... Pennsylvania

Shawn Peachey

Shianne Peachey.. Pennsylvania

Stennet Kurtz .... Nakuru, Kenya

Brant, Valerie, and Tara Newswanger .... Pennsylvania

Trentlyn Newswanger.. Indiana

Kiana Good.. Pennsylvania

Mariana Beth Martin .... Indiana